I0726995

Broken Bonds:

A Paranormal Protector Tale

Book 2 in the Heart of Stone series

DEMELZA CARLTON

This book was created with the assistance of a grant from the Western Australian Department of Local Government, Sport and Cultural Industries.

ONE

Anemone dusted off her hands. "All right, that should do it. Forty-eight hours of electrolytic reduction and by Monday afternoon, those tools will look as new as the day they were forged in the prison smithy."

Beth laughed. "Or the day they were discarded, if they're ones that came with the convicts from England. The tools they made were pretty crude, but still a damn sight better than the ones they were supplied with. It's a wonder those convicts built anything at all, let alone half of Perth and Fremantle."

Anemone shrugged. "Tracing the history of things is your job, or one of the archaeologists. I'm just a chemist moonlighting as a museum curator. Little more than a glorified dishwasher, really."

"Uh huh, sure, Dr Seaver. Last time I checked, you don't get PhDs for dishwashing."

"Boat washing," Anemone corrected her. "I did my PhD on marine corrosion on boats." Which is where she'd met Morgan, and first been dazzled by his smile. Her heart constricted in her chest. She'd never see him smile like that again.

"How are the kittens going?"

Anemone blinked, all the way back to the present and Beth's sympathetic smile. "Kittens. Yes. They've grown a lot now, big enough to leave their mum. The shelter's sending over some prospective adopters this afternoon, so I should probably get home before they arrive."

Beth's eyes turned misty. "Aw, I bet you'll

miss them if they do get adopted. Aren't you tempted to keep them?"

"Maybe. If no one wants to adopt them. But the shelter have plenty more cats and kittens for me to foster, once these find their forever homes, so it's not like I'll be alone."

"See? I told you fostering kittens would make you smile again – I saw that! My foster babies were the only thing that kept me going when Brad left me. If I hadn't had them to take care of, I wouldn't have gotten out of bed at all that first week. At least yours still have their mum – mine needed two hourly feeds. Worse than human babies, or so I'm told."

Anemone forced out a smile. Beth might know about Morgan, but she didn't know about the miscarriage, and Anemone had no desire to tell her about it today. "I wouldn't know." She pulled off her lab coat and hung it up. "Right, I'm off. See you on Monday."

Beth waved, already intent on the flaking paint she was painstakingly restoring once more.

Anemone waited for a tour group to pass, then crossed the parade ground to the gatehouse. More tourists milled about in the courtyard, but she weaved through them and headed out, with a wave of farewell to the tour guides at the gate.

The markets were in full swing, so she cut through William Street instead of braving the crowds on South Terrace before she headed down High Street home.

The barriers were still up, blocking the dug-up road to vehicle traffic, though the footpaths were fine. Full of more people than she was used to seeing, too – all enjoying the fine weather and the relaxing of restrictions. Maybe this pandemic really would be over soon, like the news reporters kept saying.

She sure hoped so.

Anemone trudged upstairs to her apartment, heading straight for the bathroom where she kept the kittens. She cracked open the door, but she wasn't fast enough to catch the dark streak that shot through before she could even get a foot through the door. One look told her who the escapee was: Bruce Wayne, mum to the litter of kittens who remained happily playing in the bathroom.

Anemone sighed. Bruce was less than a year old, and not much bigger than her three surviving kittens. She'd been a stray caught in a quarry before she was brought to the shelter, where her kittens had been born. Unlike her kittens, who were happy to be handled and fine around people, little Bruce wanted nothing to do with them.

No one would be adopting Bruce any time soon, so no matter what happened with the kittens today, Bruce would likely be staying for a while longer. But she could tidy the place up a little…

The bathroom had never been so clean and she was just brushing the kittens one last time when her phone rang.

"Mmm, hello?" she said, setting it on speakerphone so she could keep brushing little Clark Kent.

"Hi, it's Hope, from the cat shelter. I just wanted to warn you that we had a lot of interest in your kittens, with more than a dozen people wanting to come meet them. Instead of setting up individual times, I figured it would be easier to run it like a home open, so I brought all their adoption papers and a portable EFTPOS machine. If I send them up one at a time to see the kittens, would that work for you?"

Anemone swallowed. Hope would think she was silly if she refused, but this would be the first time she'd had visitors in her new apartment since Morgan died. Well, someone had to be first. Best that it was strangers she would never see again, instead of people who knew her and would give her long, pitying looks if they saw the boxes of Morgan's stuff that she hadn't been able to unpack.

"Sure. That sounds fine. Do you want to man the back door, the one to the car park? That way, I can leave it unlocked, and when I send the first person down, you can send the next one up." There. A plan. It even sounded like she was in control again, instead of…well, someone who wasn't fit to foster cats.

"Awesome. Well, I'm in the van, in the courtyard, so if you want to come down…"

The afternoon proceeded as smoothly as a well-oiled machine. Before Anemone knew it, little Peter Parker, Dick Grayson and Clark Kent were on their way to their new homes, where they'd hopefully get more original names than the ones the shelter had doled out, and she had the apartment to herself again.

Well, herself and Bruce Wayne, the furry fugitive.

Anemone sighed. She'd look for the cat later. Now, it was time to prepare something for dinner, and after she'd eaten, then she'd scour the house. She wasn't about to go to sleep with a creature loose in her house, causing who knew what kind of mayhem.

TWO

Dunstan awoke in darkness, straining his ears for the sound of her. He pushed through pitch, until he broke through into gloom, slipping through shadows in search of her.

She was here, somewhere. She had to be.

Not in the basement, where shadows swallowed the silence. Not in the foyer, where the day's dying rays lanced through coloured glass windows, staining the floor before they faded.

He stepped out onto tiles already chilled from winter's bite.

One thing was certain: he would guard his heart this time. Once he'd had the heart of a normal man, capable of love and pain in equal measure, but now he had a heart of stone, impervious to any woman's charms.

Footsteps echoed from above. Ah, she was upstairs.

Dunstan began to ascend.

THREE

Anemone threw herself down on the couch. She'd searched the place, top to bottom, twice, and she still couldn't find Bruce Wayne. What if she'd somehow managed to sneak outside? She'd be drenched and cold and probably hiding somewhere and she'd never hear the end of it from the shelter if she lost a cat. Some foster carer she was.

The weather evidently agreed with her,

hammering the windows with raindrops so hard they might have been hailstones. Anemone prayed the cat wasn't outside. She wouldn't want her worst enemy out in this.

A bloodcurdling yowl erupted, only just audible above the rain.

"Bruce?" Anemone called, heading for the stairs. Up or down? Another furious yowl had her breathing a sigh of relief – if Bruce was upstairs, she wasn't outside.

The noise grew louder with every step she took, until Anemone stepped into the bathroom Bruce had originally escaped from.

Bruce had managed to climb into the kitten enclosure, and she was nosing around it, calling for her lost kittens.

Anemone dropped to her knees. "I know how you feel, little one. I lost my baby, too. You've just got to tell yourself they're in a better place now."

Bruce flattened her ears and hissed.

"All right, I'm not sure I believe it, either, but you have to keep going. Remember to eat and sleep and do all the normal things you have to in order to stay alive. Here, let me get you some of the special food I bought..." She'd been feeding them the cat biscuits the shelter had provided, but she'd spotted the little individual seafood pouches at the supermarket last week, and somehow they'd ended up in her shopping trolley...

"It's called saucy seafood morsels," Anemone told the cat as she peeled back the lid and poured the contents into a bowl. It looked like something she might eat, and it didn't smell too bad, either. "I know food is hardly a replacement for your family, but you have to eat..."

A chill rippled down Anemone's back. Then a second one. She looked up, just in time to see a fat drop of water disconnect from the ceiling and plop into a growing puddle on the floor. No, no, no...the roof couldn't be leaking. Not on a Saturday night in the middle of a storm when no one could come to repair it.

She'd have to move the cat to somewhere else.

Anemone scooped up the little black ball of fur, which cowered in her arms like she actually trusted Anemone to take care of her. Luckily, Anemone's sweater was too thick for those needle-sharp claws to penetrate, though Bruce dug them in deep.

"Shall we shift you to the laundry for tonight?" Anemone asked. "It's dry and warm because I have the dryer on, and I can make up a nice bed for you in the laundry basket." She grabbed the bowl of food. "You can eat your dinner in there."

The drips came faster now, pattering on the floor almost as hard as the rain outside.

The cat squirmed out of her arms and leaped for freedom.

"No, come back!"

That's when the world came crashing down.

FOUR

He found her in the bathtub. She rose from her crouch, dust haloing her like an angel as she shook her head and looked up at where the ceiling should be.

Then she said a few words that proved she was definitely not an angel. He wasn't even sure what all of them meant. He almost laughed. A lady who could outswear a sailor was not someone to be trifled with.

He followed her gaze. Fireworks were going off in the rafters, and two cables that looked for all the world like that telegraph thing he'd once seen, spat sparks on the wet floor below, as more water cascaded down. Then another shower of plaster came down, dropping the end of one of the cables to the floor with it, as the other swung dangerously low.

A yowling ball of fur exploded out of the bathtub and landed on the counter beside him. The little black cat then began to rub her head against the wall, as if she knew he was hiding there.

"No, Bruce!" the woman wailed.

One of the cables dangled dangerously close to the cat.

He didn't think. He seized the nearest cable, swinging it away from the cat. Sparks sputtered against his skin, but he barely felt them. He tied the two together, so they hung well away from the floor, and turned to face the woman.

"Oh my God…how did you…never mind. I'll go shut the power off." She scrambled out of the bath and set off at a run.

She returned a moment later, out of breath and shaking the dust from her hair. "That has to be the bravest thing I've ever seen. You could have been killed. You can let go of it now. I've turned the electricity off."

He nodded. The cables had stopped sparking, which had to be a good thing. Perhaps it was time to ask questions now. "What's electricity?"

FIVE

She didn't know who he was, or where he'd come from, but Anemone wasn't going to look a gift horse in the mouth. He'd saved her life, so that was one big point in his favour. That already made him a superhero in her eyes.

She shone her torch at him, trying to get a better picture of her saviour than the one she'd seen through the flickering sparks from the torn power cables.

Actually, the first thing her torch beam landed on was Bruce, purring all over the man's feet. Bruce, the cat who didn't like anyone. Well, he couldn't be that bad if Bruce liked him.

Anemone felt her shoulders relax almost of their own accord. She took a deep breath and looked closer.

Bare toes peeped out of the bottom of his baggy pants – the sort her dad had worn when she was a kid, when those were fashionable – and ridges of muscle just rose up from there. There was something behind him, shadowed by his body, like a sort of cape. Exactly what she'd expect a superhero to wear. She wanted to lift the beam to illuminate his face, but blinding him would be rude.

So it was much more acceptable to let the light play across his abs, as she wondered what to say to Batman's younger, better looking brother.

"That has to be the bravest thing I've ever seen. You could have been killed. You can let go of it now. I've turned the electricity off."

Oh God, now she was babbling. She should be saying thank you, asking him who he was, or how he'd gotten in here.

"What's electricity?" he asked.

Anemone blinked. Was he testing her? Or maybe he had taken a jolt from the wiring and now his brain was fried. "It's the flow of charge, in this case carried by electrons through copper wiring. Probably from the coal fired power station down south, or maybe a gas turbine, seeing as it's night time now, so the solar panels won't be producing any more power until morning…"

Babbling again. He was going to regret saving her in a moment. Any minute now…

Someone pounded on the door downstairs.

"Anemone? It's Catena from next door. Are you all right?"

Bruce bolted at the sound of the neighbour's voice.

Anemone reached down and grabbed the cat before she could escape again, wrapping an arm firmly around her as she headed downstairs.

She struggled to unlock the door with only one hand. "Give me a moment. I'm trying…" Finally, she got the door open. "Um, hi?"

Up close, Catena looked younger than she remembered – like she was still at university.

"I heard you scream, and I just came to check to see if you were all right," Catena said.

She'd screamed? Instinct, surely, for she didn't remember doing it. Oh, no wonder Batman had come to her rescue. Morgan used to say that when she screamed, she sounded like a banshee heralding the death of the human race. Catena would definitely have heard it.

What had she asked again? Oh, if she was all right.

"Fine, fine." But she'd nearly died, what with water and electricity trying to mix on her bathroom floor. "Now, anyway. Some of the rain got into the roof, and part of the ceiling in my bathroom collapsed. Water and wiring everywhere. It's all right now, though. I've turned the power off at the fuse box. I'll call an electrician in the morning. After I've had a chance to clean up the mess." And finish questioning Batman. She still didn't know how he'd gotten into her house.

Anemone blinked. Somehow, Bruce had squirmed free, but instead of running, like she usually did, she was rubbing against the wall. Purring. Like she'd done in the bathroom just before Batman appeared.

She didn't remember Batman being able to walk through walls. Unless that was a special talent reserved for his younger brother…

She really needed to get back inside and ask him, now.

Anemone mumbled an excuse for the cat's strange behaviour, and tried to pick her up.

Bruce, being Bruce, was having none of it. She dodged Anemone's hands, darted between Catena's legs, then skittered around and raced back inside Anemone's apartment.

Better than racing down the stairs and into

the foyer…or worse, into Catena's apartment. It was a miracle the cat was still alive.

"Well, let me know if you need help with anything. I'm just across the hall," Catena said, heading back to her place.

Anemone nodded, and hurried to close the door before the cat decided to escape again. Once she'd locked the door, she raced up the stairs to the bathroom.

"Now, I don't mean to sound ungrateful for you saving my life and all, but I have to ask…" Anemone began.

Only to find that she was talking to herself, for the bathroom was empty. The Batman was gone.

Bruce rubbed against her foot, letting out a piteous mew.

Now that was a first.

"Let's get you some dinner in the laundry, like we were planning before all this happened," Anemone said. She collected what she needed and carried it down the hall. The cat came with her.

As the little creature noshed on her second sachet of saucy seafood, Anemone watched her. If she hadn't seen both of them in the same room, she'd almost wonder if it were possible for the cat to shift into a man. Bruce Wayne and Batman were hardly a stretch.

But no. "You're not really a Bruce, are you? After today, I think I'll call you Lucky," Anemone said.

Lucky was too busy slurping her fish to disagree.

SIX

The sea was all around her, waves swishing against the hull. No one and nothing but water, from horizon to horizon. But she had to find him. She had to, or he'd be lost forever. Lost to the sea, and then she'd be lost, too…

Anemone woke up with a start. That bloody nightmare again. Why she kept having it when she knew better than to go sailing alone, she didn't know.

But still she did what the grief counsellor had told her, because it was supposed to help. Somehow.

She was home in bed, in a sea of cotton sheets that were soft beneath her questing fingers. She took a deep breath, inhaling the faint scent of the drying lavender in a vase on the dressing table. She switched on the bedside lamp, so she could see the room for herself. Only to find Lucky, curled up and purring, at the end of her bed.

"I thought I locked you in the laundry," she said to the cat.

Evidently not. Either that or the cat could open doors.

Oh shit, what if she'd opened the door to the mess in the bathroom and tracked plaster dust all over the house?

Anemone padded upstairs, where the floor was mercifully free of dusty pawprints. The laundry door was, indeed, wide open, explaining Lucky's freedom, but Anemone could have sworn she'd closed the door before she went to bed.

Maybe Batman had come back to save the cat from durance vile. Perhaps he'd mistaken her for Catwoman, and she should have renamed her Selina Kyle instead.

No. Batman and all the other superheroes were fictional. She must have imagined the man in her bathroom.

Yet when she raised her camping lantern to light up the place, the mess was still just as she remembered it, with the knotted electrical cables tied into a net well clear of the floor. She'd seen him tie those knots, even if she hadn't seen him that clearly.

Maybe he was an angel Morgan had sent, for it could not have been Morgan himself – she'd have recognised his voice.

God, listen to her. First she was having nightmares about being lost at sea when she never sailed out of sight of shore, and now she was debating whether she'd been visited by a superhero or an angel last night. Maybe she'd gone mad.

Mad or not, this mess needed cleaning up, and Anemone knew she wouldn't be getting much more sleep, so she may as well make a start on it.

Back to the laundry for some gloves, buckets, stuff for sweeping and another couple of camping lanterns, before she set to work. She carted bucket after bucket of debris outside to the bins until they were full, and still it looked like she'd barely touched the pile. Maybe because the biggest section of intact ceiling still sat there, too big to take outside unless she broke it up or had someone else to help her.

Where was Batman when you needed him?

In a comic book where he belonged.

It was Morgan she wished was here now. He'd have waded in to help, working alongside her until everything was done. Maybe this never would have happened if Morgan was still here – he would have noticed the signs of the impending ceiling collapse, and fixed things before they got this bad.

But Morgan was gone, and he wasn't coming back, so she'd have to deal with this herself. Grimly, she grabbed the edge of the ceiling panel, and flipped it up so she could move it aside. Anemone propped it up against the wall, then turned back to the much smaller pile of debris that had been hiding underneath it. She dropped to her knees with her dustpan and brush, ready to continue, but the first sweep of her brush uncovered something brown and leathery.

She prayed it wasn't the dried corpse of some long dead rat and carefully brushed the dust away from it. No, not a rat – this leather had stitches. But it was so tiny…

With shaking hands, she scooped up her find. It was a child's shoe, so small it might have belonged to a baby or a doll.

Like her own baby might have worn, if she hadn't lost him.

Without warning, she was dropped back into a nightmare, but it wasn't a stormy sea that surrounded her this time. Instead, it was a pool of blood that she couldn't seem to stop flowing, and the pain in her midsection was like she'd been stabbed.

A desperate cry clawed its way out of her throat as she surrendered to what she knew was not only a nightmare, but a memory.

SEVEN

His heart might be made of stone, but it took a heartless man indeed not to be moved by the kneeling woman, sobbing her own heart out on the dusty bathroom floor, clutching a child's shoe to her chest.

Why, his own son might have worn just such a shoe. The memory itched at the back of his mind, but, try as he might, he could not recall what his son's face looked like. All he knew was that he had lost him.

As she must have lost her child, for who but a mother could cry in such agony?

He didn't think. He stepped from the wall and dropped to the floor beside her, before he pulled her into his embrace.

She stiffened at first, but then he said, "Cry as much as you need to, miss. There is no shame in a mother's grief."

She sniffled. "But I don't need to, that's why it's so silly. I just can't seem to stop…"

And she cried some more, while he held her, before she finally stilled.

"Will you tell me about him?" he asked. "The child you lost?"

"But I didn't really know him, or if it was a him at all. He was…I knew I was pregnant, and I was just waiting for the right time to tell my husband, until the night I lost him. Maybe I lifted too many boxes, or maybe I did too much, or maybe there was something wrong with him and he never would have survived the birth…I'll never know, but I went to the bathroom, and there was blood everywhere…I don't even remember calling the ambulance, but I must have, because Morgan wasn't home. He didn't come home. I woke up in hospital and the police were there to tell me…tell me…" She dissolved into tears again, sobbing even harder than before.

He just held her. It seemed like the right thing to do.

When she stilled again, he said softly, "I lost a child, once, too. I never saw him, either. His mother married another man, and told him he was his father, and she wouldn't let me see him…" He swallowed. He could not remember his son, but he could remember her voice, telling him to leave and not come back. "I can't imagine how much harder it must be for a mother," he finished.

She pulled away from him so he could see her face as she shook her head. "No greater than a father's grief. If Morgan had known…if I'd had a chance to tell him…he would have mourned right alongside me. We would have…we probably would have tried for another child by now, but…" She wiped her eyes. "What about your son? Where is he now?"

He spread his arms wide. "I do not know." He considered how much time had passed since the day he'd discovered he was a father. He did know, though he wished it were not so. "But I believe he died a long time ago."

She nodded slowly. "It's not natural for children to die before their parents. Wrong, somehow, as though the world had twisted on its axis and could never be the same again."

He stared at her. How could this woman read his mind? Was she a witch, or some sort of supernatural creature?

She offered him a watery smile. "Did Morgan send you?"

He shook his head. He knew no one by that name.

She gestured at his wings. "I thought, what with those wings and all, you had to be an angel, and maybe…"

He was no angel. That he knew for certain. "I'm not an angel, but a gargoyle, miss. The gargoyle protector of this building, and those who dwell here." He frowned. If this was true, and he knew it was, then surely he would remember helping her when she'd lost her baby. Yet he had no memory of the night she'd described. No memory of her at all.

Her smile turned wistful. "Not an angel, and not Batman, either."

"No, miss, I'm not a batman. I was a ship's carpenter…before…" He couldn't recall any of his past, except for the snippets of memory that seemed to rise up like flotsam before sinking again. "Before I became a gargoyle."

"And are hugs and comforting weeping women normal tasks for a gargoyle?" She ducked her head, hiding a smile. "I haven't met a gargoyle before and I'm curious."

"Miss…" No, it was missus, wasn't it? She'd been married. "Missus…"

"Doctor, actually. Doctor Seaver. I met Morgan when I was doing my PhD and he was so proud when I graduated…but you can call me Anemone, if you like. Doctor Seaver is what I make obnoxious men at conferences call me, when they try to correct me on things they know nothing about. You're telling me about gargoyles, which you know far more about than I do, so…Anemone."

A soft chirp came from the door, followed by the patter of paws as the little black cat crossed the room to jump onto his outspread wings, resting on the floor behind him. The creature curled into a ball and began purring.

"And that's Lucky," the woman added.

He reached over to stroke the cat. It purred harder.

"I'm Dunstan," he said.

Doctor Seaver – Anemone – extended her hand, like a man would. "Pleased to make your acquaintance, Dunstan the gargoyle."

Dunstan knew enough of the world to be certain that shaking her hand in a manly fashion was not something he should do. So he leaned over and pressed his lips to the back of her hand instead. He might not be a gentleman, but he knew how they were supposed to behave. "An honour, Anemone."

She folded her legs beneath her and gave him her full attention. "Now, tell me all about gargoyles."

EIGHT

When the sun rose, Anemone wandered to the ensuite bathroom to wash all the dust off, but her mind was firmly fixed in the other bathroom, with Dunstan, though the gargoyle himself had departed just before dawn, telling her that gargoyles could not endure sunlight, for it turned them to stone.

Part of her brain wondered at how easily she'd accepted the existence of gargoyles, let alone the one who could appear and disappear at will inside her bathroom, but she had to admit there were things in this world that science could not explain yet, and creatures like Dunstan were definitely one of them. And he was fascinating.

He'd stood up and done a slow twirl to show her his wings, tail and horns. His tail poked out of a hole in the back of his pants, longer and more sinuous than Lucky's tail, and ending in a sort of heart-shaped point.

His wings had looked leathery, but they'd felt softer than that, more like a stingray. Or maybe a bat. He'd told her he was made of living stone, despite looking very much like a man, which he had once been, though he had very little memory of that time.

A time before electricity, Anemone guessed.

Being stone, he hadn't actually been in much danger from the sparking electrical wiring, but he still bore some scorch marks from the sparks, and he said he had felt them hit him.

He did not live on the roof, as a statue or gutter spout, but somewhere dark, beneath the house, from which he could be summoned when he was needed. Not the basement, but…it sounded like some sort of other realm. It was unnerving to think of a gateway to somewhere else under her house – what if someone or something worse than Dunstan crawled out of it?

If anything did, he would protect her from it, he promised, but he didn't think there had been anyone there when he left. It wasn't so much an entire realm but a pocket in this one – just big enough for him.

It sounded awfully like a grave or a tomb to Anemone, but she hadn't dared say it. She knew there had been several cemeteries in Fremantle since the first colonists arrived, but none of them had been beneath her house. There had been that news article a few weeks ago, where some high school kids had dug up one of the graves behind the old asylum, and people had been joking about zombies rising from the dead, but…if there had been a zombie loose in Fremantle, someone would have gotten pictures of it by now.

He did not eat or drink, and he did not need to sleep, either. He could fly and walk through walls, though he couldn't explain how he could do the wall thing. It did explain how he'd shown up so fast when the ceiling fell in, though.

He knew nothing about the shoe, or how it had come to be hidden in the ceiling. A shoe that looked like it had been there a long time.

What she should really do is speak to someone who'd lived here longer than her – like Catena, the girl across the way. If Anemone remembered rightly, the place had belonged to Catena's grandmother, and it had been in her family for some time, maybe even since it was built. Perhaps the shoe had belonged to Catena's many times great uncle or something.

She took her time dressing, still pondering everything she'd learned in the pre-dawn hours. What she really needed to do was to talk to Catena.

NINE

Anemone had left a message for the emergency electrician, eaten breakfast, loaded the dishwasher, done every other chore she could think of, and it was barely nine in the morning. Was it too early to go next door to talk to the neighbour?

Only one way to find out, she guessed, so she headed across the landing to knock on Catena's door.

Her heart sank when she saw that Catena was still in her pyjamas.

"I'm sorry to bother you so early," Anemone began, wishing she could sink right through the floor.

Catena just shrugged. "I've been up for a while. I was about to make my second cup of coffee."

Anemone felt a smidge better. If the girl had had time to make and drink a cup of coffee… "Oh, no worries, then. Well, actually, maybe. This is going to sound really strange…"

If she told her the whole story, Catena would probably think she was mad. Batman and gargoyles and Lucky…

Catena already looked sceptical.

Just the non-crazy sounding bits, then.

"Okay, I thought it was really weird, but…while I was cleaning up the mess from last night, I found a shoe. A kid's shoe." Anemone paused as Catena's eyes narrowed. Oh, this wasn't going well. She rushed to continue, "Look, it's…it reminded me of some of the ones in the museum collection. Really old and solid. It looked like it had been in the roof for a while." Damn it, she was babbling again. Too much coffee, probably, and not enough sleep. "I'm not saying this very well, am I? I work in conservation. I don't find things, other people find them, and then they bring them to me to make sure they're preserved. Or find out if they can be preserved. Archaeology's more your area, and I remember you saying you knew the family who used to live in my apartment before I bought it…" She trailed off, then took a deep breath. "Look, you said last night to ask you if I needed help with anything. I don't really need it, it's just…there was a child's shoe hidden in my house. If you'd found it, wouldn't you want to know more? Maybe even find out who its owner was?"

Okay, now she sounded desperate, and her neighbour knew it. Lonely old widow goes mad, with only a cat for company, so she digs up a mystery and gets obsessed with it…

"Yeah, I'd totally want to solve the shoe mystery, if it was me. Give me a minute to grab my camera and some brushes and I'll be right over. I can't promise I'll be able to find anything more than we know already, but I can at least take a look and do things properly, so we have something to go on if you want to dig a bit deeper."

Anemone let out a breath she hadn't known she'd been holding. "Thank you!" She nearly hugged the girl, but she'd probably done enough hugging strangers for one day…actually, for the month…so she managed to resist.

She headed back to her apartment, considered making another coffee, then decided to brew some calming tea instead. Tea that wasn't done yet when Catena knocked on the door.

Anemone ushered her in, and guided her up the stairs.

"I stopped sweeping the moment I found the shoe, so you could see it in situ as much as possible," she said. Now she looked around, she could see all the things she could have cleaned or tidied away before inviting anyone in. She couldn't remember the last time she dusted or vacuumed, and there were cat things all over the place. What would Catena think of her?

Catena's eyes widened when she reached the bathroom, but Anemone could understand that. The place looked like a bomb had hit it. Thankfully, she didn't comment on the mess, but went straight to work instead, laying her things down and taking pictures of the shoe.

Anemone wrung her hands. She knew she shouldn't have disturbed the site, but… "I'm sorry, I found it while I was sweeping, so I picked it up. By the time I'd realised…I'd already brushed some of the dust off it, and it was already on its side, so most of the crap inside had fallen out." Babbling again…

Catena was too intent on the shoe and the surrounding dust to even glance at Anemone. "It's not like it's Tutankhamen's tomb, the sort of treasure the whole world will want to know about."

Yet she was treating it every bit like a formal archaeological investigation, with a ruler and everything. Anemone wanted to hug her neighbour.

"Is there any chance I can have a look up there?"

Anemone blinked. Catena was pointing at the roof cavity where the ceiling should be.

Why on earth would she want to go up there? It was probably full of spiders and who knew what else. But if that's what she wanted… "Uh, sure. I'll go get the stepladder."

It took her a while to find it, because she couldn't remember where she'd put it, but when she finally dug it out from one of the guest room wardrobes, Catena didn't look too impatient.

Anemone set it up under the gaping hole, and held it steady while Catena climbed up, looking askance at Dunstan's handiwork with the wiring.

How did she explain that? Without mentioning Batman or Dunstan… "They're turned off at the main switchboard, I promise. If they were live, they'd still be sparking. They're safe." She crossed her fingers that Catena wouldn't ask how she'd tied those knots without climbing up the stepladder.

But Catena seemed satisfied by Anemone's explanation, and continued up past the cables into the roof cavity.

Anemone waited while she looked around, not saying anything as she clicked away with her camera. Finally, Catena said, "Hey, Anemone, could you pass up my brushes and that ruler? I think I might have found another one."

Another shoe? One shoe was weird enough, but a whole bunch of them…what sort of people put their shoes in the ceiling?

Anemone passed up her things, then hurried to hold the ladder again, which was wobbling a bit, with Catena standing on top of it.

Without warning, a shower of debris came

down, and they both swore, then started coughing with all the dust that came with it.

Catena climbed down again. For a moment, she seemed to be staring at the wall, until Anemone realised Lucky was rubbing against the plaster. She wondered if it smelled like Dunstan.

Then she looked down at the new pile of crap that had come down from the ceiling. There was another shoe. If she couldn't already see the original one a metre away on the first dust pile, she would have thought it was the same one. She nudged it with her foot, easing it out of the dirt. "It looks like a pair."

Catena had the strangest expression on her face, like she was about to say something, then thought the better of it, and knelt down to brush the new shoe clean. She set them together on a bare patch of floor, and there was no mistaking it now – they were a matching pair. So why…?

Catena took a few more pictures of the pair, then straightened up. She snapped her brush case closed with the practiced ease of someone who'd done it countless times. "Well, I've got some pictures, and I'll do a bit of research with those. What do you want to do with the shoes?"

She wanted to give them back to their owner, but whatever child had worn these might have died of old age by now. Anemone shrugged. "I don't know. I guess I'll do what we always do in the museum when something new comes in. Bag 'em and freeze them to kill any bugs." Who knew what sort of bugs lived in that old roof cavity?

Catena nodded. "Sounds like a plan. Well, I'd best go have some breakfast, and I'll let you know what I find. And if you do need any with anything – repairs, whatever, let me know, all right? Just because we live alone, doesn't mean we are alone." She stared at Lucky.

Not with Dunstan in the building, too. "Yes. Well. Thank you. I should probably finish cleaning up in here so I can have a shower." Another one.

"Yeah, I'll need one, too, after that."

Anemone ushered Catena out and closed the door firmly behind her. Then she sank down to the floor, with her back to the door.

Shoes falling from the ceiling. Gargoyles walking out of the walls. Kind neighbours who wanted to be friends. Anemone had lived such a quiet life since she'd lost Morgan, it was almost too much for her to have going on at once.

And yet…it was, and there was nothing she could do to stop it. Actually, she should probably try calling the electrician again, in the hope he could come out today to sort the wiring. She did not want to be stuck with camping lanterns for light again. Even with Dunstan here, it was downright creepy with the house so dark. If she went to bed early, the nightmares would only come back, and she'd bet every cent she had that there'd be baby shoes in them now.

TEN

Dunstan might be confined to the walls after the sun rose, but that didn't mean he stopped watching her. When she undressed in the bathroom, he had to force himself to look away, but not before he glimpsed her reflection in the mirror.

God, she was built like a goddess. Curves in all the right places, yet small enough to envelope her in his arms to keep her all to himself, and the rest of the world away, for as long as she'd let him. He couldn't remember the last time he'd touched a woman, let alone a naked one, but it took all of his self control not to slip into that shower behind her and offer to help her wash.

He might be made of stone, but some parts of him grew harder than the rest, just like any man would, when presented with such a vision of beauty. Her husband must be mad, not to want to be with her every moment of the day and night.

He managed to get himself under control while she went to talk to her neighbour, but then she returned, and bent over to examine something on the floor.

The roundness of her behind as she bent over, stretching the fabric of her pants, showing the exact shape of the perfection these modern clothes did nothing to conceal…

He almost stepped out of the wall, sunlight be damned, to fall to his knees in worship.

He would not give her his heart, but other

parts of his body had no such scruples.

Her young neighbour might have been a witch, too, for more than once she'd fixed her gaze on the wall as if she knew he was there. The cat kept rubbing against his leg, too, even through the stone wall.

A sensible man would have descended into the darkness, and fallen into oblivion to await Anemone's summons.

Dunstan, being a glutton for punishment, chose to stay where he could see her. He could not explain it, but he felt it was the right thing to do. Even if it was seven kinds of wrong to want another man's wife so desperately.

If only he could keep his desires under control…

ELEVEN

All of the afternoon and most of her paycheck later, Anemone had the lights back on.

"When you get the ceiling replaced, give me a call and I can install a new ceiling light for you. But you'll need a carpenter to replace the ceiling and probably a stonemason to deal with the storm damage, and repair the walls or this will only happen again. Don't know where you'll find one of those, though. These heritage buildings…" The electrician shook his head. "Anyway, when you find someone to do the work, give me a call, and I'll squeeze you into my schedule. The good news is your insurance company might cover some of the costs of the repairs, so call them on Monday."

She thanked him and saw him out.

When he'd driven off, she sat at the dining table, with her head in her hands. She wouldn't know where to start in finding someone who specialised in repairing heritage buildings.

Actually, that wasn't true. The staff at the museum would know. The museum was in one of the earliest convict buildings in Fremantle, so they'd have a list of contractors who knew how to take care of century-old falling apart structures. And then there was the prison heritage officer, who complained daily about how hard it was to keep the crumbling limestone from falling down around their ears.

Tomorrow she'd make a few calls. Something would turn up.

Nodding to herself, she moved to the

kitchen. She usually spent Sunday evenings preparing meals for the rest of the week, and today would be no exception. Especially now she had all the power back on. This week, she'd planned to put a Hungarian style goulash in the slow cooker, so she set to work on that one first, as it took a night and a day to cook, and needed stirring occasionally in the first couple of hours.

Hmm, she was almost out of smoked paprika. She jotted it down on the shopping list, then checked for what was next on the menu. Ah, chicken and sweetcorn soup. That took a bit of time, but it froze well and she could take some of it for lunch during the week.

The chicken was browning in the pan, Lucky was happily slurping up the meat scraps and Anemone paused to add hoisin sauce to the shopping list.

"What are you cooking? It smells like Singapore in here."

She could only stop and stare. Under the

bright kitchen lights, he could have been a statue – Michelangelo's David, only wrought in limestone instead of marble, and wearing pants. Every bit of him that she could see was lean, hard muscle, including his wings. Maybe not the tail, though. Or the horns.

But the horns would give a girl something to hold onto if she straddled him, Anemone thought idly before she caught herself. She hadn't thought about another man like that since…before Morgan died.

And Dunstan had saved her life and comforted her when she needed it most. He did not deserve to be objectified in the middle of her kitchen, for goodness' sake.

Even if he would make a magnificent statue. Without the pants, of course.

Anemone shook her head to get the inappropriate images out of it. "It's Asian style chicken and sweetcorn soup, or it will be. Right now, it's just chicken breast pieces stir-fried in hoisin, soy and oyster sauce, with a bit of Shaoxing wine. You can have some when it's ready, if you like, though it'll probably be another hour or so, because I'm making a big pot to last the week."

He shook his head. Not a statue any more. "I'm living stone. I have no need to eat."

Yet he had a sense of smell, which surely meant he could taste… "You could just taste it. Stick your tongue in a spoonful of it, maybe?"

"The smell is sufficient. It reminds me…"

"Of Singapore, you said. When did you go there?"

He shrugged, and the ripple went through his shoulders and down his wings. "I don't remember."

Of course. "What do you remember?"

He shook his head. "Nothing good."

"You must have some good memories," she persisted.

"If I do, I don't remember them." He bowed his head. "Please forgive me, Miss…Anemone. Doctor Seaver. I am poor company tonight. If you do not need my protection, I will…go…"

"Not back to where you were before." It came out sharper than she'd intended. Anemone wet her lips. "I hate to think of you stuck in some place dark, like you described, waiting for a summons. I don't even know how to summon you. I mean, what if…" Now who couldn't finish a sentence?

"Then I will go up to the roof. I will not be far." Before she could respond, he stepped into the wall and was gone.

Anemone blinked. Having a gargoyle in her house would take some getting used to.

TWELVE

A fine mist of rain was falling when Dunstan reached the roof, but the droplets merely rolled off his wings, so he ignored it. Maybe the chill would be a good thing, in contrast to her warm, welcoming kitchen. He'd known her two days. He could not possibly have come to care for her in that time.

His heart was stone. Hard and impermeable and indestructible. Not at the mercy of some woman, even if he was her protector.

The way she'd talked of tongues and tasting…

He certainly hadn't been thinking about soup. And now, even in the winter rain, the images of what he wanted to do to her would not go away.

The way she'd looked at him when he first came into the kitchen…just for a moment, her eyes had seemed to smoulder, and he'd remembered she was a married woman, not some virgin maiden. She knew what it was like to bed a man. A very lucky man, who wasn't him. God, he was willing to bet she was amazing at it.

Swearing, he spread his wings and in one powerful downsweep, he was airborne, arrowing into the wind in a desperate attempt to wash the dirty thoughts from his mind.

THIRTEEN

Thankfully, no more of the ceiling came down before Anemone had to head into work on Monday morning. The café across the road was open, and they did better coffee than the stuff they had in the office, so she decided she had a few minutes for a detour. And a mocha. Or maybe a cappuccino…

"Good morning," the girl behind the counter greeted her, with the beaming smile only an early morning barista could pull off.

Anemone returned it, all the same. "Morning. I'll have a...can you do me a mochaccino, please?"

"Sure."

"You want a muffin with that?" A second woman, closer to Anemone's age, stepped out of the kitchen with a steaming tray of muffins. They smelled divine.

Hell yes. Anemone's mouth watered. "What kind are they?" she hedged.

"White chocolate and macadamia, raspberry and coconut, and of course, the triple choc. The raspberry coconut one's gluten free, too. More of a friand than a muffin, really."

It was definitely the raspberry and coconut one she could smell. "Raspberry, please." But the others looked so good... "And one of the others, for later."

"Light or dark?"

Today, she wasn't sure. "Whichever one looks best," Anemone said.

The younger girl started making her coffee.

"Have you seen the Mothman?"

"The what?" It had to be some new movie or TV series.

"The Mothman." The girl pointed at the screen behind the counter, where a video of a man in a cape grabbed a woman, then disappeared, before the short video played again. "We're offering a month's free coffee for anyone who can get another video of him. That was right outside here, you know."

Anemone stepped up to the counter, to get a closer look at the video. He looked a bit like Batman, or Dunstan, at first glance, but whoever he was, he was definitely bulkier than Dunstan. "It looks like Batman to me."

The woman dropped her tongs with a clatter. "He looks nothing like Batman! Batman has cat ears and a cape. This guy has wings, and those things on his head are antennae – completely different."

"Or horns," Anemone said without thinking. They did look like Dunstan's horns. But it couldn't be him.

Now the girl peered up at the video. "You know, they could be horns. Wings, horns…do you think he might be a demon instead?" She shivered. "I think a Mothman sounds a lot safer."

The woman blew a raspberry. "Demons and angels don't exist. That guy does, though, and he's bringing in scores of customers in the evenings, hoping to catch a glimpse of him." She glanced at her watch. "Are you okay to manage the place alone while I take Rory to school?"

The girl grinned. "As long as no demons show up, sure."

"Rory!"

A little girl who might have been about five skipped out of the kitchen, her high ponytail bouncing with every step. Anemone didn't know they made school uniforms that small. "Can we go now, Mum?

"Yes, honey. Are you sure you'll be okay here by yourself, Rochelle?" the woman asked.

Rochelle rolled her eyes. "I'll be fine, mum."

"She's my mum, not yours," the little girl snapped, setting her hands on her hips.

"Sorry, Rory. I'll be fine, Tacey," Rochelle said.

Tacey nodded. "I'll be back soon. Then I'll make a start on the sandwiches."

The little family left, leaving Anemone alone with Rochelle.

"Have the pandemic restrictions hit you hard?" Anemone asked.

Rochelle shrugged. "Me, no, but Tacey, who owns this place, had to cut down her opening hours, and let all the casual staff go. I think she's done okay with the government support, but it's great for her that things are opening up again. Of course, getting the word out that we're opening evenings again is a bit slow…hence the Mothman contest." She waved at the screen. "It's bringing in a nice crowd, but I don't know how long that will last unless someone gets another picture of him." She lowered her voice. "Between you and me, I wouldn't put it past Tacey to hire some guy to dress up in a Batman costume, if the numbers start to drop again. I mean, the free coffee is a nice incentive, but if no one sees him again…" She looked up, hope lighting her eyes. "You haven't seen him, have you?"

It wasn't Dunstan. It couldn't be. Slowly, Anemone shook her head. "And even if I did see this guy, any blurry, shaky shot I got on my phone camera wouldn't be worth showing anyone. I'm terrible at taking pictures. Good thing I can afford to pay for my coffee habit, because I won't be winning your contest any time soon."

Rochelle set her coffee on the counter and popped a lid on top. Then she picked up the tongs. "One raspberry friand and…what was the other one you wanted?"

"Whichever one looks best," Anemone repeated. Because they all looked so good.

Rochelle peered into the muffin cabinet. "Oh, I found the perfect one. It looks like a chocolate one, all dark on top, but it's pale underneath. Like Tacey poured the last of each batch of muffin mix into the same case, so it's half and half. Light and dark together – perfect for someone who can't decide." She bagged the muffins and set them on the counter next to Anemone's cup. "Tomorrow, you can tell me which half you liked better."

Tomorrow? Anemone couldn't remember the last time she'd deliberately gone out for food before today. And yet…she wasn't entirely averse to the idea. Maybe…maybe she could stand to spend time with people again. "Tomorrow," she agreed, before she left for work.

FOURTEEN

Anemone had asked around at work, but no one could tell her a good carpenter to come and help her fix her ceiling. In fact, if she found someone suitable to do repair work on heritage properties, her colleagues would consider hiring them, too. Especially if they knew anything about restoring convict era limestone.

So, just before she went to get lunch, she

called the Maritime Museum.

"Hi, Conservation Department."

"Emily?"

"Anemone?"

"Oh my God, I was just going to call you. They need to put in some new moorings off Rottnest Island, and the Board absolutely refuses to go ahead with it unless a full impact assessment is done on the shipwrecks and the dive trail, and they're insisting they need you on the assessment team. I tried explaining that you don't work for us any more, that you're on secondment to Fremantle Prison, but because your name is on the last set of wreck condition reports before the dive trail went in, they won't accept anyone else. Please, will you do it?"

Anemone wished she could say yes, but… "I'm really not comfortable on boats any more, Emily. And shipwrecks…"

"I know, I know, but these are over a hundred years old, and more coral than hull. And it's not like we'd be actually sailing or anything. It's at Rottnest. We'll be anchored really close in to shore, and all you have to do is watch the monitors while the divers do all the work. Please, Anemone."

"I'm really busy at the prison. They've just got funding for some preservation works and the archaeology team has found all sorts of caches beneath the floorboards in the cells. Plus they're about to start work on the Commissariat, which dates back to the 1850s, and…"

"There isn't anyone else. We've looked. Everyone else who's even half as qualified or as experienced as you is either interstate or overseas. Normally, we'd fly someone in if we have to, especially with another department picking up the bill, but we can't even do that with the borders closed. Plus, they have to get those moorings in before October, or they lose the funding, and works are scheduled to start next month…you're our only hope. Honest. And I swear to you, nothing bad will happen. It'll be the safest ship that ever bobbed about on the calmest seas imaginable, spitting distance from shore, all in daylight hours. The site's too rough to dive in all but the calmest weather, so if there's even the slightest hint of a storm, we won't be going out. Please, Anemone. I will personally cook you dinner every night for a month if you do this."

Anemone had to smile at that. "You can't cook."

"That's not true! I've never burned a lasagne yet!"

"That's because you only cook frozen lasagne, and you put it in the oven for the exact time it says on the packet, and you use a lab timer to make sure you remember to take it out on time."

""It still counts as cooking. I've met men who couldn't even do that!"

Anemone sighed. Yes, so had she. Morgan hadn't been much of a cook, either, but if it was about building things or fixing things or anything that went on the water, he was wonderful at it. He probably would have given the ceiling a go on his own. With all his work on replica boats, he might have known exactly what to do, too.

But Morgan was gone, which was why she needed to find a carpenter, and why she was now working with the prison museum team instead of the one at the Maritime Museum, and why she was going to hate every minute she was on the boat.

"If you promise not to cook me dinner for a month, I'll do it," Anemone said. "But only if my boss agrees."

"Believe me, at the consulting rate they're paying, your boss won't turn this down. He'll be able to afford a temp to cover your job and pay you, with money to spare. Right, let me give you a run down on the schedule and which wrecks we'll be inspecting…"

The rest of the phone call involved Emily explaining the entire project brief, while Anemone scribbled notes down as fast as she could. The more she heard, the more she knew there was no way she could back out now. No one knew those sites better than she did —

she'd dived them almost daily during the previous survey. It had been one of her favourite projects at the Maritime Museum — second only to the *Batavia* relics at the Houtman Abrolhos.

Conserving artefacts at the prison was interesting and all, but underwater archaeology was like entering an entirely different world.

"So, see you at the boat ramp, first thing next Monday morning!" Emily said, and ended the call.

It wasn't until Anemone had set the phone receiver back in its cradle that she realised she'd forgotten to ask Emily about a carpenter.

Shit.

FIFTEEN

When Anemone arrived home that night, she was greeted by the welcoming aroma of the goulash – now ready to eat. "If you weren't just a mindless machine, I could totally fall in love with you," she said to her slow cooker.

A mew from near her feet drew her attention to Lucky, and the now empty bowl she sat expectantly in front of. Sighing, Anemone took care of Lucky's dinner before dishing up her own.

She'd picked up a nice sourdough loaf on the walk between work and home, so she cut a couple of slices to sop up the stew. Then she considered the bottle of wine on the bench, leftover from what she'd poured into the goulash. Though she didn't usually drink alone, a glass of it would go well with dinner. She reached up for a wineglass.

"Good evening, Doctor Seaver."

She set two glasses down on the counter. "Good evening, Dunstan. And please call me Anemone." She waved at the glasses. "Would you like some wine? Or some goulash? I have plenty."

"Gargoyles do not need to eat or drink, Anemone."

She blew out a breath. "I know, you've told me, but it doesn't feel right to be eating in front of you...or worse, drinking wine in front of you, without offering to share it with you. Especially as you've been here all day, with the cooking aromas to tempt you into tasting it.

What do you do all day, anyway?"

"When I am not beneath the house, awaiting your summons, I hide within the walls. Watching," he said.

She lifted her wineglass to her lips and sipped. Oh, that was a lovely red. Probably too good to use in cooking, but it was too late now. She'd definitely drink the rest. "What do you watch?"

It couldn't be her – she'd been at work.

"Your cat found a bug this afternoon, and it was amusing to watch her hunt and catch it."

Well, that hadn't changed, in all the time since Dunstan was born right up until the present cat video craze.

"And after that? Or before it?" she prompted

He hesitated, then said, "Many people walk past your home on the pavement outside. They wear different clothing than I am used to, and some of them stare at small screens they hold in their hands, instead of where they are going. It is most – "

A knock at the door interrupted him.

"Hold that thought. I'll be right back," she told him, heading for the front door.

SIXTEEN

Anemone opened the door to find Catena standing there. "What can I do for you?"

Catena said, "I thought you might like to know what I've found out about your shoes."

Shoes? Oh the ones that fell out of the ceiling. "That was fast. Come in. We're just finishing up dinner."

Anemone threw the door open wide, but Catena shrank away. "I didn't know you had company. I can come back later, or another day, if you like."

She'd said we, hadn't she? For a moment, Anemone considered telling her neighbour about Dunstan, then decided against it. If she hadn't seen the gargoyle with her own eyes, she'd think she was mad to tell such a tale. Instead, she said, "Oh, no, it's just me and the cat. Come in and see."

Just as she'd suspected, Dunstan had disappeared again. Almost like he really was a hallucination.

"Oh, what is that?" Catena exclaimed.

Anemone scanned the room, but the girl's attention was fixed on the bubbling slow cooker. Anemone breathed a sigh of relief. "A Hungarian style goulash. It takes about two days to cook, so I do a huge batch and freeze it in, or I'd be eating it for every meal for a week. Here, I'll get you some." She served it up, and cut some more bread for Catena, setting a place for her at the bench.

Catena looked torn. "Oh, I couldn't…"

"Sure you can. There's heaps. It's the least I can do, if you've found the owner of my mystery shoes."

Catena avoided her gaze. "Yeah, that might not be as easy as I thought…"

Briefly, she explained about the horrific practice of foundation sacrifices, burying bodies or personal items in the foundations of buildings to protect them.

Anemone only half listened, for her thoughts had immediately wandered to Dunstan, and his grave beneath the house, or whatever it was. It sure sounded like he'd been a foundation sacrifice.

But…witches here in Fremantle? What next?

Anemone sighed. "So you think a witch put the shoes there?"

Catena choked, and it took several minutes of coughing while Anemone fetched her a drink before Catena could answer.

"I don't know about a witch," she began cautiously, "but it looks like the shoes were probably put there as part of some fertility or protection ritual. Whether they actually do anything is anyone's guess, and I suppose it depends on what you believe."

Protection and fertility. Two things she could definitely do with more of. Well, not the fertility right now, but maybe one day… "So I should put them back, then?"

Catena looked shocked. "If you believe in that sort of thing, I guess it can't hurt. If they weren't doing anything, then it shouldn't really matter."

Anemone thought about it for a moment. Perhaps they'd been put in the wrong place, and were somehow responsible for her miscarriage in that very bathroom, her first night here.

"There are more things in heaven and Earth than are dreamt of in your philosophy," she said softly. If some badly performed ritual were responsible for her child's death, that it wasn't something she'd done, or overdone…

"From what you've said, it seems they're

supposed to be hidden near the hearth, not up in the roof. I might put them back in one of the fireplaces instead, up the chimney. Seeing as they weren't doing any good where they were." And one day, if she should ever be lucky enough to have someone come into her life who might consider raising a family with her…

Anemone shook her head. No. She couldn't think about that now. "Is there anything else I should do? You mentioned protective marks?"

Catena seemed reluctant to say much more. "Well, in the other buildings where shoes and things were found, there was always more than one, in different places. And marks carved or burned into walls and doorways and hearthstones. As if the people who believed in such things thought the more protection they had, the better, right?"

Catena evidently didn't believe in the supernatural, or any of this. Well, she was young, and maybe she was right. Good thing Dunstan had come to her aid and not Catena's

– her neighbour probably would have dismissed him as a figment of her imagination. Then again, it was hard to argue against the existence of someone who'd definitely saved her life. Besides, Anemone preferred to keep an open mind.

Protective marks...she'd heard something about those at work today. Someone at the prison had believed in them, too. So Anemone wasn't the only one...which meant there really might have been witches among the early colonists at Fremantle.

"I know it was certainly the case at the prison. The main buildings are pretty much pristine, with very little graffiti on the walls except where the prisoners got permission to do artwork, in the last days before it was closed. There's not a single convict mark from construction on the main cell block, or the gatehouse. But the walls are a different story. Especially the north wall, which blew over in a storm the year after it was built." That was the wall that needed the most frequent repairs, too. Strange.

She looked up to find Catena staring at her. "A storm blew the limestone wall over? Seriously? Those walls have to be thicker than the walls of this place, and about as high. To think a gust of wind could just tip that over…wow. Just…wow. It must have made an almighty bang. You'd have heard it for miles."

Kind of like her ceiling crashing down on the floor. "Well, they rebuilt it right away, seeing as it was a prison wall, and it's probably stronger now than it ever was now. Of course, nothing lasts forever. It's overdue for repairs, crumbling all over the place. If you ever come across anyone who has experience with Victoria era limestone walls, or century old jarrah rafters, can you give me his number? It seems the leak that brought down my ceiling was in the walls, not the roof, so I'd want to hire him first, but they want someone like that at work, too. The prison's applied for a grant to cover the costs, but there's no way they'll be able to spend the money· if they can't find someone capable of doing the work."

Catena and her grandmother had lived here longer than she had. If they'd had any repair work done, surely she'd know someone…

Catena hesitated. "Well, I do know someone who did some repair work on my walls recently. I'll see if he's available. I wouldn't know where to start looking for a carpenter, though."

Anemone thanked her, and soon found herself alone in the kitchen again.

But not for long.

SEVENTEEN

"If you need the services of a carpenter, I am only too happy to assist."

She would never get used to the way he stepped right out of the wall like that. "Not only are you the only gargoyle I've ever met, but now you're a gargoyle carpenter? There can't be many of those in the world."

"I don't know any other gargoyles, carpenters or otherwise, but I assure you, I know my trade. I built more ships than I can remember, and your rafters are no different to an upside down ship. Once I am finished, your ship will be as watertight as any of the king's warships."

Anemone had to laugh at that. "The Queen. We have a queen, and she has a consort, though probably not for much longer, seeing as he's over ninety. Do you remember who your king was?"

Dunstan stared at her. "I had no king. Only a queen, too."

"Well, I suppose that narrows things down. Only which queen was it? Victoria, Elizabeth...I believe there was an Anne between them, too. Then again, you do have a Scottish accent. Perhaps it was Mary Stuart. Which would explain why you don't know much about electricity..." She stopped babbling when the crease in his brow grew too pronounced to ignore. "Let me guess, you don't remember that, either?"

He raised his hands in surrender. "I might

not remember the name of my queen, but I do remember how to work wood. Only procure the right materials, and I shall repair your roof, better than the day it was first built."

Anemone sighed. If it was Morgan, she wouldn't argue. She'd just let him do it, and then call in a professional if he told her he couldn't do it. She didn't know the first thing about fixing ceilings, and Morgan had built a boat, too. Well, half of one, seeing as he'd never quite finished it. Never would, now.

"There'll be no procuring anything this late in the evening. Maybe tomorrow, and I wouldn't have the first idea what the right materials might be, so I'd need your help on the procuring part, too." She eyed him. "I suppose we could order the materials online and have them delivered. That might work."

"If you feel that is best." He ducked his head.

Morgan would have argued about wanting to examine the wood first, and doing his shopping in person. Dunstan was evidently a different kind of…oh.

"You don't know what ordering things online means, do you?" she asked.

He shook his head, horns and all. "I do not, but you seem to, and if this is the best thing to do, then it is what we shall do."

Her head hurt just thinking about it. She had no idea what she was doing, let alone what was best.

"Let's deal with that later. I think I've earned dessert tonight. What do you think…profiteroles?" She opened the freezer door and peered inside.

And right there, front and centre, was the pair of baby shoes, double bagged, like Snow White in her glass coffin for all to see. For a moment, Anemone forgot to breathe.

She had to get the shoes out of here. Somewhere she wouldn't have to look at them.

She seized the bag and turned to Dunstan. "Change of plan. Catena said these should have been placed under the hearth, or in the chimney somewhere. That way, they bring good luck and fertility or something. With your magical ability to walk through walls, can you find somewhere suitable to put these? Because with all the bad luck I've had this last year, I could really do with some of the good stuff."

He edged the shoes out of the bag. "I shall find the perfect place for them." Then he and the shoes vanished into the wall.

EIGHTEEN

There were two fireplaces on this floor, and neither had a fire lit in them, but neither seemed like the appropriate place for a fertility charm. If there'd been a hearth in the kitchen, that would be the place, for that's where she spent most of her time.

Faint memories tickled the back of his mind. He'd done this before, for someone else. Not the same shoes, though, and it had definitely been a cooking hearth, in a dark cottage that had none of the wide windows and bright lights of this place.

No, if Anemone wanted a fertility charm to be effective, it must be placed in her bedchamber, for surely that is where her husband would take her to conceive a child.

It's where he would take her. He'd lay her down on the bed, those blond curls spread across the pillow, her eyes laughing as she begged him to make love to her as he kissed every inch of her, over and over, until he could take no more of her pleading, and he gave her what she wanted. What he wanted, too, deep inside her, his wings wrapped around her to angle her just right, so that she cried out his name, not once, but over and over, as he pleasured her from dusk until dawn.

If…she was not already married to another man.

When her husband returned, Dunstan would ask her to dismiss him back to the darkness from whence he came. He could not bear to see or hear them together, to see her face alight with happiness as she beheld another man.

A man, not a monster.

She wanted her husband to make love to her, and she wanted the monster to put this fertility charm where its magic might give her a child to hold in place of the one she lost. And he, obedient monster that he was, would grant her wish.

The tiles in the hearth in her bedchamber were firmly glued together, leaving no space for even this tiny pair of shoes to hide. The chimney, of course, was a different matter. There were all manner of nooks and crannies, all the way up. One even had a rat skeleton in there, sitting on a piece of paper with markings on it that Dunstan didn't recognise. Witch runes, he imagined.

One particular nook was about Anemone's eye level, if she stood in front of the fireplace. He brushed away the dust and soot, then carefully set the shoes there.

Perhaps they would bring her the child she wanted. For a moment, he dared to imagine a little girl, with Anemone's golden curls, running about the house like a tiny whirlwind, a storm that swept all before her, until her mother scooped her up for a kiss and a cuddle, her own face alight with joy.

Dunstan hoped he would one day see it, just as he imagined. That these shoes or the spell cast on them or some other magic in the world would bring her the happiness she craved.

He emerged from the wall, to find her eating ice cream in the kitchen. "It is done," he said.

She dropped the ice cream bowl on the bench and threw her arms around him. "You are wonderful! Thank you so much!"

Dunstan closed his eyes, and for just a moment, allowed himself to enjoy the bliss of her soft body against the hard stone that was his own. He ached for her, more than he'd ever ached for any woman. If she only said the word, husband or no husband, he would…

Anemone backed away, a beaming smile still on her face. "I'd offer you ice cream, but…"

"A gargoyle has no need for food or drink," he said woodenly. Or intimacy, or love…

He might be made of stone, but that didn't stop him from wanting things he couldn't have.

"Right. So, how about I turn on my laptop and we can shop for ceiling stuff? Bunnings might be closed, but they have a pretty good website…"

Though he didn't understand most of that, Dunstan still found himself nodding. Whatever made her happy, he would give to her, without question.

It was a good thing she would have no need for his stone heart.

NINETEEN

Dunstan and online shopping definitely did not agree with each other, so Anemone had closed her laptop and gone to bed, worrying about what would happen if she took the gargoyle into a hardware store. Maybe it would be easier to try and find someone else to do the job.

Someone without horns and wings…

But work kept her too busy the next day to

make any phone calls, and all too soon she found herself headed home, squinting into the dying rays of the sunset, until her heels clicked across the cool green tiles of the foyer, and she could shut the rest of the world out for a moment.

"I have a list of the tools and materials I will need," Dunstan greeted her as she dropped her keys in the bowl beside the front door. He held out a sheet of paper covered in neat copperplate.

If the sheet hadn't been torn from her shopping list pad on the fridge, it would have fitted in perfectly with some of the early prison records. Perhaps his queen's name had been Victoria, or maybe that's just when he'd learned to write.

For all the neatness of his handwriting, the list meant little to her. He'd have to come to Bunnings, whether she liked it or not. If anyone remarked on the wings or the horns...they'd just have to say he was a cosplayer, trying out a new costume before the next convention.

She looked him up and down. She hadn't been to a convention in years, but even she would have wanted her picture taken with someone as gorgeous as Dunstan. Except for those pants.

"You can't wear those. They've been out of fashion for more than twenty years. You'll need shoes, too. Morgan might have something that will fit you…" She beckoned for Dunstan to follow her into her bedroom.

All Morgan's clothes were still exactly where he'd left them, in the cupboards and drawers they'd brought from the previous house. Even though she knew in her heart he wasn't coming back, she still couldn't bring herself to get rid of them. Silly sentimentality, she'd told herself every time she said she was going to give his things away, but each time she'd balked before actually taking anything out.

And now her sentimentality didn't seem so silly, if it could help Dunstan fix her ceiling.

"Shirts and pants are in there, and shoes

should be on the racks below them. Socks are in there, and anything else you need should either be in those drawers or that wardrobe," Anemone said, pointing to each in turn. She swallowed. "I don't know how you'll get a shirt on over the horns and wings, but the more like a normal human you look, the easier this will be."

"I understand."

Then he hunched over, and Anemone didn't realise what he was doing until suddenly his pants were sliding down the most perfect backside she'd ever seen and…

"I'll wait outside then, okay?" She didn't wait for an answer.

Outside the door, she buried her face in her hands. Never in a million years had she thought he'd go commando under those pants. At least he'd had his back to her, or she'd have gotten an eyeful of gargoyle peen.

After what felt like forever, but was definitely long enough for her burning cheeks to cool, Dunstan cleared his throat. "Does this meet with your satisfaction?"

Anemone took a deep breath and entered her bedroom. Her breath caught in her throat. For a moment, it could have been Morgan standing there, a ghost returned to life, until he turned to face her. Then, her mouth turned dry as a beach in summer. While other parts further south turned decidedly damp…

Morgan had never looked that good in a pair of fitted chinos and a button-down shirt. His clothes had always hung off his lanky frame, but Dunstan's muscles filled everything out perfectly. It was like he'd stepped out of a menswear catalogue.

"The shoes are too big. I grabbed a couple of extra pairs of socks, which helped," he said.

She let her gaze drift downward, forcing herself to look at his shoes. "They look fine to me."

Dunstan grinned. "These clothes are very fine, and so are the shoes. Finer than I am used to. I will take care not to damage them. I dare not button the cuffs, but if you permit me, I could roll up the sleeves…"

He demonstrated, revealing his muscles again.

If he kept this up much longer, her knickers were going to catch fire. Or melt. Or something.

"You are very fine," she muttered, then clapped her hand to her mouth, hoping he hadn't heard.

Perhaps he hadn't, for he turned away to scrutinise his reflection instead.

That's when it hit her.

"Your…your wings. What happened to your wings?" she gasped out.

He turned, and she realised that wasn't all that was missing.

"And your horns?"

"You said you would like me to look like a normal human. This is what the men of your time look like, as they hurry along the street outside. You do not wish your shopping partner to look like a monster, and so, I am as you see." He waved a hand at his more ordinary form.

"You can do that? Shapeshift like that?"

"I can take any form you desire, to better protect you," he said.

She took a longer look. He still had the same muscles everywhere, but without the horns and the wings and tail he looked…lesser, somehow. As flat as the magazine this man belonged in.

But he would blend in just fine in Bunnings, which was what she wanted right now.

"Right, shall we go, then?" she asked.

TWENTY

Anemone was silent all the way to the goods store, and likely would have remained silent all night, if she had her way, for something evidently troubled her. She would scarcely even look at him.

Dunstan suspected he knew what the problem was, and, consequences and his own feelings be damned, he needed to be certain.

So as they left the warehouse, with her car

full of all the things he needed to make the repairs to her house, he asked, "Will you tell me about the man whose clothes I wear?"

She stared at him for a long moment, then turned her eyes back to the road. "You mean Morgan? My husband? We met at the yacht club when I was doing my PhD, researching corrosion in boats. He taught me to sail, and let me experiment on his boat. Well, one of them. He lived aboard an old fishing charter boat when I met him. I think he spent more time on the water than he did on land. Truth is, I think he loved the sea more than he did me, or anyone, really. I understood. I mean, no one can compete with the whole ocean, and I could love it right alongside him. That's why we picked this apartment. It was close to the yacht club and the ocean, and you could see the water from the windows…or walk down to the boat. It was close to my work, too, and he was fascinated by the things the maritime archaeologists discovered. Historic boats…he wanted to build one, you see, a perfect replica that we could sail around the world one day, or to somewhere, at least. He started one, but he never did finish it." She sighed. "I guess he never will, now."

She did not speak of their love, or passion. Perhaps they had been married long enough to lose the blush of first love.

"Is he away at sea a lot?" Dunstan asked. For long voyages away would explain his absence now.

She shook her head. "That's just it. He was never out for long, and he always wanted me to come with him, not stay behind. Well, when he wasn't taking day charters, or giving someone sailing lessons. So when he didn't come back…I knew something was wrong. I still think it was Janus's boat, which was never properly repaired, and always in need of more paint. The other guys said it was a freak wave that hit them and capsized the boat, but Morgan would never have let that happen. He knew the ocean better than any man alive. He wouldn't have…"

He recognised the reasoning of a woman in denial. One who believed her man would return, and keep whatever promises he'd made to her, when time and tide waited for no man…or woman, either. "So your husband has left you?"

For the first time, he dared to hope.

Anemone frowned. "Yes. And…no. Morgan never would have left me willingly. We were happy, and planning…all sorts of things for the future. More than anything, he wanted kids, so he could teach them to sail, and love the water the way he did. The way we did, or at least before…" She shook her head. "Part of me wants to believe he's still out there somewhere, that he's alive and one day he'll come back to me. Maybe that's why I still keep all his things, just in case, even though I know he's not coming back. The coroner even declared him dead, lost at sea. He wouldn't do that unless he was sure. But no one ever found the boat, or his body. All the other guys aboard were rescued. Just…not him…"

A widow. His hopes soared, as his heart plummeted. He'd known too many wives widowed by the sea. Seen the way they stared at the water, as if wishing it would give them back the man they loved. The father of their children.

"I am so sorry. My deepest condolences for your loss. To lose your husband to the sea is a terrible thing."

Anemone sniffled, then wiped her tears away with one hand, then the other, never taking her eyes off the road before them. Even the sky wept along with her. "Thank you, I think. You must think I'm so silly, a weeping widow, even though he's been gone almost a year now. And no matter how much I wish he would, he won't be coming back. He won't."

Dunstan reached out and laid a hand on her arm. "There is nothing foolish about mourning the loved ones we have lost. If I could remember any of my family, I'm sure I would mourn them, too." A faint memory, the ache of loss, squeezed his heart for just a moment, then was gone. He had loved and lost, but who, he could not say.

An eternity passed in silence, or perhaps it was just a moment, but the next thing he knew, Anemone was saying, "Right, we're here. I'll go turn the courtyard lights on, and we can bring everything inside. I'll have to look up standard rates for roof carpentry, so I can pay you fairly for your work. This is your house, too, and probably has been for longer than I've been alive, but it's my roof, so I'm paying for the work."

She seemed to expect him to argue, but Dunstan had too much on his mind to do any such thing. First, he would fix her ceiling, just like he'd promised, and then…maybe he'd have wrapped his head around her being not a happily married woman, but a widow.

TWENTY-ONE

When the sounds of hammering and sawing started, Anemone set down her tea and sidled up to the bathroom to take a peek. It turned into a longer look, then outright staring.

Dunstan didn't even notice, he was so intent on his work.

Sawdust covered him from head to toe, turning his skin gold, for he'd changed back to his old pants, and both the shirt and shoes were nowhere to be seen. His tail wrapped around the piece of timber he was shaping, as his wings fanned the sawdust away from him.

He was a vision in polished bronze, or he would be if he stood still.

Her mouth was far too dry. The sawdust, that must be it. Except other parts of her were anything but dry, and no amount of sawdust could turn her on.

She managed to drag her eyes off him, only to end up crouched in the hallway outside, breathing hard.

She was lusting after a monster. An actual, honest-to-god monster. With horns. Anemone buried her face in her hands.

What would Morgan think if he knew? What would he say?

The tears came, but only a few, and then her eyes were as dry as her mouth. Morgan was gone, and no amount of crying or dragging his memory to her attention would bring him back. If Morgan were here, he'd be fixing the ceiling, and Dunstan wouldn't be doing it instead.

So what if she was lusting after Dunstan? He was hot, and that she could acknowledge that without feeling guilty meant that maybe she'd moved to a different stage of mourning. Acceptance, maybe, or whatever it was.

Wherever Morgan was, if he was anywhere, he'd be proud of her, keeping herself together after he was gone.

Anemone forced herself to her feet. She had nothing to be ashamed of. Well, maybe ogling the gargoyle who was being so kind to her…

Anemone cleared her throat. When Dunstan turned to her, his eyebrows raised, she said, "Thank you for doing this. We never did discuss payment, but I will of course pay you whatever is the going rate."

A grin spread across his face, slow and sexy and…

Her knickers weren't melting. They were sublimating, going straight from solid to thin air, evaporating in the heat of his gaze.

"Oh, there's only one thing I want in

payment for this," he said.

Her mouth shouldn't be so dry. It shouldn't. "And what…what is that?" she managed to say.

Another grin that would have destroyed her underwear all over again, if it wasn't too late for them already. "I think you know."

She swallowed. "I do?" She sounded so breathy, so needy, so….

So help her. If he asked, she'd give it to him.

"I want you to trust me to finish your boat." He ducked his head. "If I finish this to your satisfaction, I'd like to see your late husband's boat, so I can show you what I can really do."

The boat? He wanted to see the *Sloepie*? "Of course." She cleared her throat, hoping her voice would come out normal. "Of course." That was better. "When you're done here, I'd love to show you Morgan's pet project. If you know anything about North Sea fishing boats and can finish her, that would be wonderful."

And a whole lot more sensible than some of the things she'd been thinking. Of course he was more interested in the boat than her. Men were all the same when it came to their passion projects.

"I'll head off to bed then, all right?" she said.

"Sleep well and sweet dreams. I'll keep working. Gargoyles don't need sleep." He picked up the saw again and went back to work.

TWENTY-TWO

Anemone lay in bed, but sleep didn't come. Even though she couldn't hear Dunstan working upstairs, she couldn't stop thinking about him. Couldn't get the image out of her head, with all those golden muscles…

She couldn't deny the man…no, the gargoyle…was good with his hands. If he could work a woman's body half as well as he worked wood…oh, just the thought of his hands on her…

Her hands strayed south. Well, why shouldn't she take care of herself? She couldn't remember the last time she'd done this, and it wasn't like Dunstan or anyone else would hear her. She might be a widow, but she was still a flesh and blood woman, and she deserved some pleasure in her life.

And if she imagined it was his hands on her instead of her own…what was wrong with that? It wasn't like he'd ever know.

Though that knowing look in his eyes as he'd said she knew what he wanted from her…she was soaking wet just thinking about it.

He'd look at her like that as his hand slid down her tummy, peeling away her knickers, before slipping a finger inside her, to confirm just how wet she was.

Of course, his fingers were thicker than hers, and longer, too, so she'd need two fingers to even approximate the feeling of one of his inside her.

She closed her eyes.

No, he'd want her to look at him. He'd command her to look at him, and when she obeyed, he'd reward her, placing his thumb firmly on that little bundle of nerves, circling, circling, faster and faster…

Until she cried out for joy.

But Dunstan, with his knowing eyes and skilful hands, would never stop at one orgasm. No, he'd want to pleasure her again and again…and not just with his hands.

TWENTY-THREE

"Dunstan!" Her desperate cry reached his ears as clearly as if she'd been beside him. It took him only a moment to slip through the walls to where she was.

To where she was splayed across her bed, her hand between her legs, and the expression of utmost rapture on her face.

She did not need his help. She was…she was…

He'd done his share of pleasuring women in the past, but he'd never seen a woman doing such a thing to herself. And he was certain he'd never seen anything as erotic as Anemone giving pleasure to herself.

Dunstan yearned to step out of the wall, to join her, to replace her hand with his own, to hear his name on her lips again…

"Oh, Dunstan!" She shuddered as an orgasm gripped her.

Wait, what? Had he imagined it, or had she called to him?

She was breathing so hard, her breasts were heaving beneath her thin nightgown.

He could not move. Like the sight of her had turned him to stone, with no sunlight required.

Glorious. Goddess. Angel. Irresistible. Paragon.

Please.

He couldn't even think in sentences any more. Just words to describe the perfection before him. She only had to say the word, and he would do anything she asked. Her protector. Her paramour. Anything and everything she wished. Desired. Demanded…

"Dunstan, oh, Dunstan!" Her voice ended in a sob, as she withdrew her hand, slick with her essence. She lay there for a moment more, taking one, huge, shuddery breath, before she released it, and her whole body relaxed.

She rose from the bed, the wanton goddess gone, as she padded to the bathroom to wash her hands. A moment more and she was back in bed, curled up beneath the quilt, her blond curls strewn across the pillow.

And while he ached to join her with an intensity he couldn't shake, in the back of his mind was one chilling thought: even though she'd cried out his name, she hadn't needed his help for any of it. She didn't need him at all.

It was a long time before Dunstan could move again, and even longer before he could drag his gaze away from her sleeping form. An age passed before he could return to the bathroom to finish the task she'd set him, but he knew if he lived for a century, he would never forget the look of sheer bliss on her face as she breathed his name like a prayer to heaven.

TWENTY-FOUR

The next morning, Anemone slept through her alarm – something she never did – and she didn't even have time for breakfast before she had to leave for work. Then, when she arrived, she was greeted by the happy news that Luke's wife Bella had gone into labour, three weeks early, and he was taking paternity leave from today, so instead of just being an adviser on some of the metal conservation works around the prison, she'd been bumped up to project manager, hiring and supervising the contractors.

Then she'd discovered that the next stage on the Commissariat project had started early, and seeing as Luke was the lead on that, too, someone had slipped that portfolio in with the others on her desk and the archaeologists urgently wanted to discuss some of the unusual things they'd found under the hearth in the old kitchen…

It was already dark by the time she trudged home, the antique lights in the foyer sending their smoky glow across the tiles to entice her up the stairs to her sanctuary. The one place where no one would demand anything else from her, because she lived alone.

Only…she didn't any more, did she?

Lucky greeted her at the door, chirping and twining around her legs as she herded Anemone toward the kitchen and her food bowl.

Wrestling with the deceptively named easy

to open foil pouch of cat food took forever, not to mention spilling some of the sauce on her hands, followed by all the handwashing she had to do to remove the fishy smell from her fingers. By the time she was done, Anemone just wanted to collapse on the couch with a packet of Tim Tams, and not bother with dinner.

"Would you like to inspect the bathroom, to see if I have done the work to your satisfaction?"

She whirled to face him. "You've finished already?"

He ducked his head. "I worked through the night, then boarded up the window to keep sunlight out, so that I might continue working through the day, too. I swept up the sawdust while I was waiting for you to come home, though you'll have to tell me where to put it. You don't seem to have a midden heap, and as your privy seems to be full of water, I didn't know..."

Anemone shuddered at the thought of

having to call a plumber to deal with a sawdust-blocked toilet. She didn't need anything else to go wrong with her house. "I'll take it down to the bins out the back," she said, following him upstairs.

The ceiling looked as good as new. Better, maybe, seeing as she couldn't remember what it had looked like before. The bathtub, however, was still full of debris and now, sawdust. No long, luxurious baths until she dealt with that mess. Anemone sighed.

He must have heard. "If you show me where to dispose of all this, I'll see to it tonight, after you're asleep."

That didn't stop her feeling guilty. It was her bathroom, after all. Surely she should be the one to clean it. "If you're sure…"

He nodded eagerly. "Of course. I want you to see how well I work, so you'll trust me with your husband's boat."

Ah, of course. She'd forgotten about that. "Well, the ceiling looks good, but you should probably see the boat before you agree to do anything with it. It's meant to be a replica of the first European ocean-going vessel built on Australian shores. The museum received word of some documents found a few years ago, detailing the construction of the boat, and when I told Morgan about it, he wanted to know everything. Apparently, one of his ancestors built the original boat, and he'd always been fascinated by the *Endeavour* and *Duyfken* replicas..." Damn it, she was babbling again. "How about we go for a walk to the yacht club so you can see what state he left it in? I'll pick up some fish and chips for dinner on the way back."

He smiled. "You wish to walk out with me?"

She blinked. That was an old-fashioned way of saying dating, wasn't it? Like Elizabeth and Darcy dating. "Sure. It's definitely safer than going out at night alone."

"Do not worry, Anemone. I will protect you."

She believed him.

TWENTY-FIVE

Anemone pulled back the blue tarpaulin covering the boat. "Well, there it is." She did not appear impressed by the half-finished hull.

Perhaps in the dim light she could not see it as clearly as Dunstan could. It was a small ship, easily twenty yards long, not some one-man fishing boat, like he'd expected. "How many men travelled aboard the original boat?" he asked.

Anemone scrunched up her nose, something she did when thinking. "Uh, I think there were about a hundred survivors. Morgan kept saying there was a deck and a cabin and flags, but he couldn't build those until he finished the hull and got it into the water. That's the way his ancestor did it, and he intended to do everything the same way, as much as possible."

Dunstan nodded. A ship this size could fit that many people with supplies. If her late husband had finished building it, and rigged it properly, it wouldn't have looked out of place in any port Dunstan had visited. Here, amid the sleek, modern craft that Anemone called yachts, it was a warm slice of reality in a sea of shining metal and glossy white hulls. Of the hundred or so vessels riding gently at anchor in this sheltered cove, only one of them wasn't gleaming white.

"I could finish this ship for you. Make her seaworthy, if you have the plans and the timber to do it. This will take more than a night, though. Perhaps weeks of work, as the beams need to be shaped and bent, and all the other things that need to be done to make it watertight…" Dunstan took a deep breath. "I could even take you out for a sail in it when it's finished."

Anemone laughed. "You sound like Morgan, my late husband. More like I'll take you for a sail. I don't believe you have your skipper's ticket, while I do. I need it for work, even if I don't use it much any more."

A woman ship captain. He'd never met one, though he'd heard they existed. Pirates, mostly, not respectable ladies like Anemone. And yet…he was not against the idea.

"I would be delighted to go sailing with you, any night you name," he said.

She stared at him for a moment, then said, "You know, I haven't been sailing since before Morgan died. And afterward, I didn't want to. But now…a twilight sail sounds wonderful. Let me check the weather forecast. When there's a clear night."

"Even when it's finished, a ship this size will need a crew larger than just the two of us," he began.

Anemone laughed. "Oh, I won't believe this ship is seaworthy until I see it actually floating in the water, finished."

Dunstan drew himself up. "If you permit me to undertake the work, I will finish it, upon my honour. Even if I have to take it apart and reassemble it, plank by plank, your husband's ship will be as good as any trading vessel that ever plied these waters, or any other. Give me a month, and you shall have your ship."

She cocked her head to the side. "I take it back. Now you don't sound like Morgan at all. I think he enjoyed the building of the ship more than the idea of it ever being finished, and sailing. It was about the project, and the crafting, walking in the shoes of his ancestors. The journey more than the destination. You are a very different man."

"I, too, take pleasure in my work, or at least, work well done. But once you have built a dozen such ships, which I did before I had finished my apprenticeship, let alone achieved mastery of my craft, there is more pleasure in completing a job, and knowing it was done well, for there are plenty more waiting. Now the real triumph is when you're forced to repair a ship in a storm while it's at sea, working feverishly to save all the souls aboard, as well as your own, so it doesn't sink. A man who is not swift and sure at such a time would have died on his first voyage, not travelled the world, as I have." He knew every word to be true, yet he had no memory of even a single place he'd visited. No matter how hard he tried, his mind was frustratingly blank about his past.

She didn't seem to have noticed his distraction, for her own attention was turned to the small screen she held in her hand. A phone, she'd told him, though he still didn't understand how such a thing worked. "Well, it looks like Friday night will be a good time for a twilight sail. A clear night with enough of a breeze that we might not need the motor much."

There was no way he'd have the ship finished on Friday. Nor would he have time to find a crew for her. Dunstan opened his mouth to disappoint her.

She must have read his mind. "Not in this tub. We'll take Morgan's and my little yacht. Well, I guess it's just mine now. That one there." She pointed.

Dunstan chuckled. Of course, it was the one non-white boat, but he wouldn't have called it small. It had a cabin, an aft deck, and a mast that towered high above the varnished timber. In sunlight, the wood would glow with warmth, unlike the blinding white monstrosities on either side of it. If he'd had his pick of any boat in the cove, he would have chosen that one.

"I look forward to it," he said, and meant every word.

"Me, too." She looked surprised. "Now, let's get back to the fishing boat harbour so I can grab dinner before the fish and chips shops close. I'd offer to buy you dinner, too, but…"

"Gargoyles do not need sustenance," he finished for her.

"No, or sleep, but they do need something to do, when protecting me is too boring a job. I mean, it's not like I'm out risking my life every day, needing saving every other minute."

Dunstan thought of the last time she'd called his name. When she had most definitely not needed him. "I believe you do not need me at all, and if you chose to dismiss me back to the darkness from whence I came, you would be just fine. You are a remarkable woman, Anemone Seaver."

She turned to stare at him in the darkness. "If you want to go, I won't keep you. Whatever gargoyle thing makes you my protector, I'm grateful, don't get me wrong. I like having you around, and the ceiling and now maybe the boat…I'd be happy to keep you around as long as you want." She took a deep breath. "Or maybe I just don't like saying goodbye. I mean, the last time I said goodbye to Morgan, he never came home..." Tears glittered in her eyes, then on her cheeks.

Dunstan folded her into his arms. So soft, and yet so strong. Anemone was unlike any other woman he'd ever met. "I will never leave you, unless you wish me to. Even then, I will only be a call away, awaiting your summons."

She laughed. "A gargoyle booty call. That sounds wrong on so many levels, though I'm sure that's not what you meant."

Dunstan did not understand, but rather than call attention to his ignorance, he chose to remain silent.

"Right, dinner! Ooh, I wonder if they still have that fish and chip ice cream..."

Surely no one could make ice cream in such a flavour. Times could not have changed so much.

"Don't make that face, Dunstan. If you tried it, you'd love it, too. It's kind of like maple bacon. Salty and sweet, and perfect together, even if it sounds crazy when you first hear about it."

"I do not need sustenance. Or ice cream."

"Yeah, but I bet you want it…"

He wanted more than he dared tell her. But he suspected she already knew.

TWENTY-SIX

What with Luke away and the prospect of being loaned to the Maritime Museum on Monday, Anemone was caught up in a whirlwind of work that was only beginning to wind down on Friday afternoon. Perfect timing for her to finish up the last of her paperwork and leave on time to go sailing with Dunstan.

Of course, that's when the archaeology team

trooped in, carrying a whole lot of boxes. Anemone looked around desperately for Beth, only to remember that Beth had left early for a dentist appointment. Sue, their admin officer, only worked school hours so she could pick up her grandkids from school, which meant Anemone was the only one left in the office.

"Uh, can I help you?" she asked, looking doubtfully at the boxes.

The woman she assumed was the lead archaeologist – she had more grey in her hair than the others – set her box on Anemone's desk with a decisive thump. "Tell Luke everything's here, like he insisted it had to be this week. He said everything needed to be logged and catalogued in the prison's collection before we could move it offsite. We have two PhD students starting on Monday, so they'll be coming to collect it all first thing Monday morning."

Which meant someone had to catalogue all their finds before the weekend was over, Anemone finished in her head. And the only someone left was her.

But surely they didn't need everything. If there were two students, each one would have a different focus for their project. "Which items will they need on Monday, so I can prioritise those?" she asked.

The woman's eyebrows flew up. "Just the ones in that box...and that one...and the one Katie's carrying."

So, less than half. She could make a start on them now, and if she worked tomorrow, too, maybe she could get the job done in time. "Put them down on Luke's desk, then, seeing as he's away, and I'll get started."

She reached for the first box, which was full of stuff that had been stashed under the floorboards. Inwardly, she sighed. There wouldn't be any sailing for her tonight...if she made it home before midnight, she'd be lucky.

Several hours later, Anemone finally gave up and called Beth.

"Huh...hullo?"

"It's Anemone. The archaeology team

dumped pretty much all their findings on my desk a little after four o'clock this afternoon, and it all needs to be catalogued by Monday, when their new PhD students start. I can't do it all myself. Can you come in tomorrow to help?"

"Doh…doh worry about it. Juh…juss leave it. I'll handle it muh…Monday. You know as well as I do that puh…dee candidates don't start work right uh…away. Lit reviews and things happen first. Go home. Drink."

Anemone couldn't help but laugh. "How'd the dentist appointment go? It sounds like your face is still numb."

"Said wisdom tooth has to go. Could have gone to hospital or he said he could take it now. I said…now…not sure if I'll be as happy when this stuff wears off. Gave me some pills, though. The good stuff. Can't catalogue stuff or

oppy…operate…heavy…sheen…muh…mach inery on drugs. Prison policy."

Anemone wasn't sure if she'd understood

half of that, or if that half had made any sense, but she tried to piece it together anyway. "So…you want me to stop now, and let you do the rest on Monday, after you're not on drugs for your wisdom tooth extraction?"

"Yep. And drink. Have a drink for me. I'm on antibiotics. Just in case. Can't drink."

"Right. Got it. Go home and drink."

"For me."

And for herself, too, Anemone thought as she shouldered her bag and switched off the lights. She definitely needed a drink after this night's work.

TWENTY-SEVEN

After dinner, obedient to Beth's orders, Anemone carried a bottle of whisky and two glasses up to the roof. Dunstan followed her, carrying the apple pie he'd plucked from the oven with his bare hands, despite her protests.

"I'm sorry I'm too tired to go sailing. After hauling all those boxes around, I'm not sure I have the strength to hoist the sail, let alone steer the boat. Maybe tomorrow, if the weather holds?" she said over her shoulder.

"I'm happy to go sailing whenever suits you. Even tonight. If you are too tired, then I shall do all the work, while you lie on deck and let the waves lull you to sleep. I shall carry you home if you do not wake when we dock."

She had a sudden vision of him flying across Fremantle, carrying her home in his arms. She'd want a picture of that, if only to remind her that it had actually happened.

She must be tired. Any sane, thinking person would be worried he'd drop her, or fall out of the sky. But she trusted him enough to know he would never drop her. Hell, she trusted him enough to let him into her house. She even trusted him with Morgan's boat construction project.

But she did not yet trust him to sail the yacht she and Morgan had bought together. They'd taken their wedding pictures aboard that boat, and she wasn't sure she'd ever be able to relinquish her bond to the *Sea Witch*. She trusted him with her life because he'd saved it, and she trusted him with Morgan's boat after what he did with the ceiling, but his sailing skills…she knew nothing about those. And if the *Sea Witch* was all she had left of Morgan…no man would take it from her while she still drew breath. And god help the gargoyle who tried.

"Tomorrow," she said, clinking the bottle and glasses down on the table. "The weather will still be good, and we can go as soon as the sun's down, to enjoy the twilight as well as the stars. Tonight…let's just sit here for a bit and look at the stars." She leaned over and poured two glasses of whisky. "And you're going to join me in a drink, because spirits are mostly inhaled anyway, and a good bottle of Laphroaig can sear even a gargoyle's nose hairs, I'll bet."

Dunstan reached for a glass, then grabbed the bottle instead. "I know this name. I've seen it, approaching from the sea. This is from where I grew up, though I never could drink it. I preferred Ardenistiel whisky. They took water from the same spring, but while Laphroaig was more medicinal, Ardenistiel was what my mother used to drown our fruitcakes and Christmas puddings in. Even without the pudding or cake, it was dark and sweet, the best thing to drink on a cold winter's night."

"You remembered something," she breathed. "Do you remember when? Or how to spell that, so I can look it up? Maybe if I knew how long you've been a gargoyle, I could help you remember more from your past."

Dunstan dutifully spelled out Ardenistiel for her, and she tapped it into her phone.

"It was next door to the Laphroaig distillery in the 1820s, but it closed in 1868. That's…not possible. Are you really two hundred years old?" Even as the words left her lips, she knew it had to be possible. A man who didn't know about electricity had to have been from a time that far back. Queen Victoria's time.

Dunstan shrugged. "I must be. If I wasn't a gargoyle, I'd be dead."

So would she, because he wouldn't have

been there to save her. She suppressed a shudder, then reached for her whisky. "Then shall we drink to long life?"

Dunstan sat on the chair opposite her, and took a glass. He raised it to his nose and inhaled deeply, almost as if he intended to snort the contents instead of drinking them. "Some things do not change, even after two hundred years." He raised his glass to touch it to hers. "To your good health and a long life." And then he drank, gulping it down as though it was water and not whisky.

Anemone took a careful sip, followed by a second. She didn't have a fireproof stone throat. Nor could she sit out here in the winter air without rugging up. She dragged a blanket out of the box and draped it around herself, then reached for the pie. "Do you want half?" she asked, even though she knew the answer.

His eyes were dark shadows, but she knew he was staring at her. "If I didn't know better, I would think you are trying to tempt me."

She dug in with the spoon. "Why, are

gargoyles like fae, but in reverse? One bite of human food and you're stuck in our realm, serving humans forever? Is that how you became a gargoyle?"

He stayed silent for a long time. Finally, he said, "I do not remember how I became a gargoyle."

The first bite seemed to explode in her mouth. She hadn't had an apple pie this good in ages. She'd have to go back to that bakery. "So it could have been an apple pie. Eve tempting Adam with the fruit of knowledge and boom, you're a gargoyle, sworn to protect her."

"My name is Dunstan, and I never knew a girl by that name." He shook his head. "But I do not deny I have been wronged by a woman, for is it not written in the good book that a woman released original sin into the world?"

Anemone laughed. "Not any good book I've read. If you mean the bible, a book written by men, and twisted by more men throughout the centuries to tell people how to behave…yes, I believe they lay the blame for bad things at Eve's feet. As if one woman, and a fictional one at that, is to blame for all the bad things men have done throughout the ages. I'm pretty sure it wasn't a woman who taught a man how to rape, or oppress women."

"You sound like one of those women who march in the streets in America, shouting about women's rights and equality."

A blush coloured Anemone's cheeks, which she hoped Dunstan couldn't see in the darkness. "I might have marched in a protest or two during my university days. The world has changed a lot since you were a boy, but I think more change is necessary. We're not quite there yet. I mean, workers' rights, women's rights, civil rights…don't even get me started on LGBT rights or climate change. I think people just want to live their lives and be happy, to not be made to feel like lesser beings to some dickhead in power, but for everyone to do that…or even the majority of people to do that…" She gulped down some of her whisky. "I wouldn't even know where to start. I'm a chemist and a museum conservationist, good with rust and how to undo the damage. Global politics…it might as well be rocket science or brain surgery, it's so far beyond what I know."

"And I am a gargoyle carpenter. I know about wood and ships, leaving the leading of the world to those who know far more than I do. I can only raise a sail, not a whole revolution, and I knew men who were in Paris who saw with their own eyes that revolutions do not end well for anyone." He poured himself another glass of whisky, and tossed it back.

Anemone finished the last bite of pie, but it did not sit comfortably in her tummy. Too much talk of dark times and politics. "Can we not talk about how bad the world was, and still is? If anything were open, and I wasn't so tired, I'd suggest we go to a pub and listen to a live band, or maybe go dancing."

Dunstan leaped up onto the table, narrowly

missing her plate. "We could dance here. Put on some music, Anemone, and I will dance with you."

Anemone reached for her phone, and found the playlist she'd put together for some members' party at the yacht club. It was a mix of songs from the last fifty years, so it wouldn't have anything Dunstan would know, but…

"Oh, I know this one! Dance with me, Anemone!"

To Anemone's horrified fascination, Dunstan began to dance the Macarena. As if he'd done it a hundred times before. Complete with the sexiest butt wiggle she'd ever seen.

"Fuck me," she breathed. Now where had he learned to do that?

TWENTY-EIGHT

The moment the song began, Dunstan's body moved almost of its own accord. Though he had no memory of it, he knew this song, and the dance steps to go with it. Perhaps Anemone did not, for she did not accept his invitation to dance with him.

Very well. He would dance on his own, and show her how it was done. He felt her eyes on him, even as he turned and jumped with the beat. She couldn't seem to look away and the heat of her gaze was enough to melt stone.

Well, if she wanted a show, he'd give her a show. Dunstan stripped off his shirt and extended his wings. With one downbeat, he rose into the air above her, catching a beam of moonlight as he began to wave his arms again. When his wings grew tired, he landed on the ledge where someone had placed a small, fat gargoyle statue, and continued the dance, every movement wider, more pronounced. Until it came time to jump, and he used his wings to lift him into the air, higher than he could jump, before dropping down for the next sequence.

On the street below, a girl stood in the door to the café, holding her little screen up as if to block her view of Dunstan's dancing.

Perhaps he was being a bit vulgar…

"Should I stop?" he asked Anemone. Only her opinion truly mattered.

"Only if you want to," she said.

Dunstan considered for a moment. "Then can you play that song one more time?"

Anemone smiled. "Sure."

TWENTY-NINE

After Anemone spent the afternoon checking over the *Sea Witch* and making sure she was fueled up and seaworthy, sunset couldn't come soon enough. Of course, it was probably wise to grab a bite to eat while she was waiting, seeing as Dunstan didn't need to eat.

The gargoyle had impeccable timing, appearing in the kitchen just as she closed the dishwasher on her dinner dishes.

"You ready for some sailing?" she greeted him.

He grinned. "Either that or more dancing."

She'd dreamed about him dancing last night. Only in her dreams, it wasn't just the shirt that had come off. She'd woken up so hot and bothered that she'd been forced to take care of herself again before she could go back to sleep. If Dunstan knew how badly she lusted after him…

Anemone shook her head. "Sailing. Definitely. I've spent all afternoon getting the boat ready. This will be my first sail in far too long. We're doing this."

He inclined his head. "Then we can dance together another night."

Oh, yes please. She managed not to say the words aloud, turning away to fill a cooler with drinks so he wouldn't read them on her face.

"Right, shall we?"

In no time at all, they were motoring past the yacht club pens, and out of the harbour.

"This sure beats waiting for the tide,"

Dunstan said, peering over her shoulder.

That it did. "That tells you the depth, and those are the most recent charts," she said, pointing.

"What powers the engine? Is it steam? Where is the funnel?" Dunstan asked.

"Octane, with about ten percent ethanol, which is the standard fuel mix at the yacht club. What with ethanol being a solvent and all, I try to get fuel without ethanol, but Morgan was the one who usually organised that, and I'm a little out of touch on where to get premium fuel at the moment." The look of bewilderment on his face reminded her that he was a carpenter, not a chemist. "Are you familiar with hydrocarbons?"

He shook his head.

"Coal, kerosene…oil? Octane is a fuel oil, sort of, only highly refined. My car runs on it, too." He'd travelled with her in the car to and from Bunnings, but never asked about how that worked. Maybe he'd encountered cars before, likely whenever he'd learned to dance the Macarena. Only he didn't remember. "The fuel is burned inside the engine cylinder, instead of using it to heat steam. But it still drives the engine. I know the chemistry involved, but if you wanted the technical specifications, I could find some schematics online when we get home…"

He just kept shaking his head. "Remarkable."

"We can turn off the motor and hoist the sails when we're clear of the port, and out of the main shipping lanes. Container ships stop for no one. Well, when you're that big, I imagine it'd be hard to slow down, let alone stop."

"Container ships?"

Anemone gestured toward the freighters anchored offshore, waiting for their turn to come into port and unload. In the waning light, they would soon be little more than hulking shadows on the horizon. "The cargo ships. We still import a lot of things from overseas, even if we export a bunch of stuff, too. Mining resources, mostly, from the northern ports, and agricultural products from here and the southern ones. The borders might be closed to keep this stupid virus out, but cargo still comes through."

"But no more sails, except for…this is a pleasure craft, is it not?"

A craft she and Morgan had taken a great deal of pleasure in sailing. She'd missed this. "Yes. Commercial boats all have engines of one kind or another."

More headshaking. He looked sad. "The world has definitely changed."

They'd reached open water, far enough away from Gage Roads. Anemone switched the engine off. "Not everything. There's still wind and water and waves, and if you know how to hoist a sail…"

Dunstan definitely did know how to sail. Even with her as captain and him as first mate, they worked together seamlessly, like they'd sailed together forever. Morgan had preferred to be captain most of the time, and Anemone had never argued, but now, at the helm of her own boat…the freedom felt exhilarating. No wonder Morgan had wanted it so much.

The breeze caught the sails, sending the *Sea Witch* flying across the waves.

THIRTY

Anemone tied the boat to a garishly yellow buoy beside a pile of submerged rocks, then brought out the bag she'd carried aboard at the beginning of the evening. "Can I interest you in a drink? We finished the whisky last night, but I brought a couple of bottles of water and some beer, if you want one."

Dunstan shook his head. The whisky last night had burned its way down his throat, just the way he remembered, but it hadn't brought with it the kind of intoxication a man wanted alcohol for.

And what with the way Anemone had handled the boat, sailing as skilfully as any experienced sailor Dunstan had known, he was already well on his way to being intoxicated by her presence alone. If his stone heart had been capable of love, he'd be in terrible danger with Anemone.

"Is there some significance to this spot?" he asked.

She waved at the rock. "These rocks are a good fishing spot, hence the mooring, because it's a popular one, but it's also just far enough offshore to see the stars clearly. See?"

Indeed he did.

"It's also the halfway point on some of the yacht club social races, because it's the perfect place to turn around. One turn around the rock, then headed for home. Sometimes we'd volunteer as race officials, and head out here early in the day, and just float around until the race was over. Morgan used to set up a couple of lines to see if he could catch anything, but he rarely did. There's a pod of dolphins that swims around here, and the occasional sea lion. Not that it took more than one sea lion to make sure you couldn't land a fish. Those things are fast."

"So this was a special place for you and your husband." Yet she'd brought him here, instead of coming alone.

"Yes. No." Anemone sighed. "I liked it, because it was peaceful. Just us and the waves and the sea life, you know? But Morgan didn't like being an official. He wanted to race, to pit himself against the others, but also against himself. And…this will sound crazy, but sometimes I think he saw the ocean as his nemesis. Like they were locked in a lifelong battle, him and the water. I guess I should have expected that one day the ocean would win, because one man is no match for the whole ocean, but it was such a big part of who Morgan was. More like a lifelong rivalry, I guess, not a battle, because the ocean never seemed to notice him. Until the day it took him for its own."

A faint roar caught his ears, growing louder until Anemone evidently heard it, too.

"More night fishermen, I guess. Like I said, it's a good fishing spot," she said, pointing across the waves as she raised what appeared to be a pair of spyglasses, bound together. "Yep, recreational fishermen for sure. Ones with more money than sense, judging by how fast they're going. Professionals would never waste fuel like that, unless someone else was paying." She offered the spyglasses to Dunstan.

He peered through them, soon finding the noisy craft. It was larger than the boats in the yacht club pens, but it appeared to be hollow underneath. "It looks like one of those Pacific Island fishing boats with two hulls, only writ large and polished up like it's supposed to be a royal pleasure barge or something."

Anemone laughed. "Morgan talked about

trading in the *Sea Witch* and getting a catamaran, though a smaller one than that, I'm sure. They're faster, and have more space on deck. When the settlement came through on selling our old house, I figured it was only a matter of time before he came home with the details of exactly which cat he intended to buy, but by the time the buyers settled, he was already gone." She reached up. "Better get the lights on, so they can see us and the warning buoy. Wouldn't want that thing running aground on a rock. The repair bill would be more than our boat's worth."

A string of small lights ignited, outlining the yacht in a warm glow of a thousand candles with not a flicker among them.

Anemone caught him staring. "They run on electricity, and they're all LEDs, so the whole thing's powered by a couple of batteries. If you want to know how it all works, when we get home, I can…"

Dunstan held up his hand. "No. I'm not sure I would understand, anyway. I am a carpenter, not a scholar. It is enough that the lights illuminate. Let their working remain a mystery. I am content."

He was, too. He stretched out on the deck. He could lie here all night, just looking up at the stars.

Or he could, until Anemone let out a string of foul language that would blister the ears of even the coarsest sailor. She turned on a light much brighter than the others, which she began to wave in the direction of the approaching vessel, which wasn't slowing down.

Now Dunstan understood her issue. The fools aboard the catamaran evidently hadn't seen them, and they were headed straight for them.

The roar of the engine became so loud, he couldn't even hear Anemone's shouting. And still they kept coming.

He had only one thought – he had to save her.

THIRTY-ONE

"Wankers!" Anemone screamed at the catamaran as they swerved, sending a wave of water to swamp the poor *Sea Witch*.

Maniacal laughter rang out from the boat as they sped away, raising their drink cans to her in mock salute.

Only then did she realise that she was no longer standing on the deck of the *Sea Witch*, but several metres up in the air, with Dunstan's softly beating wings on either side of her, holding them both aloft.

She stared at him in wonder. "You saved me. Again."

She threw her arms around his neck and kissed him. For a man made of stone, his lips were surprisingly warm, and his tongue was…everything she wanted it to be. If she wasn't mistaken, that devilish tongue of his was doing the Macarena in her mouth.

Reluctantly, she pulled away. "You can probably put me down now." The *Sea Witch* was awash, but it wasn't so low in the water that a bit of bailing wouldn't sort the problem.

"I will go after them, and see that they pay for what they did. This is an act of war, and I will not allow them to get away with it!" Dunstan declared.

Anemone sighed. "No, it's just a bunch of drunken wankers, playing with their expensive toys. With no other witnesses, there's nothing anyone can do about it. It's better if you help me bail the water out, so we can sail home. So much for a relaxing evening sail."

"But this is unacceptable! You could have been killed!"

"Between our life jackets and the EPIRB, the Volunteer Sea Rescue guys would have found us, no worries." Not to mention the life raft that would have inflated. Still would, if she didn't get the water out of the boat now. "Help me, please."

Grumbling, Dunstan grabbed a bucket.

They were soon headed back to shore, too busy sailing the boat to discuss that kiss. Which was probably for the best, Anemone decided.

THIRTY-TWO

"Anemone!"

She'd barely stepped out of her car before she was enveloped in a hug so tight it'd make a python proud.

"Emily?" Anemone mumbled through a mouthful of the woman's coat.

"Of course, silly. I thought you wouldn't come. After the news yesterday..." Emily pulled away and ducked her head. Whatever the news was, it couldn't be good.

"What news?"

Emily's eyes widened. "You mean you haven't heard? It was at the entrance to Fishing Boat Harbour, right outside. Some politician's boat sank. The rescue divers were all over it yesterday, and they said it looked like the boat had run aground on some rocks, and it was taking on water when it limped back into the harbour, but it was so badly damaged it sank before it reached shore. One of those big luxury boats, too, like the Rottnest ferry only smaller. Here, they took pictures when they refloated it. They had to, or no one could get in or out of the harbour, and the fishing fleet was up in arms, ready to move it themselves if someone else didn't." She pulled out her phone, tapped at it a few times, then held it out. "The guy who owns it is being investigated for corruption now. Apparently even a politician's salary isn't enough to cover the costs of a boat that size. It's been impounded in the drydock."

Even when it was being hauled out sideways, Anemone couldn't mistake the wankers' boat from Saturday night. She zoomed in on the hull she could see. It looked like someone had thrown rocks at it, or, more likely, thrown a few punches with stone fists.

She'd have to ask Dunstan about it when she got home.

"Was anyone hurt?" Anemone asked.

"Not that I heard. A bit wet, maybe, or a few scrapes climbing up the rocks to the road. Why? Did you know them?"

Anemone shook her head. No, she didn't know them, and she didn't want to. And if all they'd lost was their boat and a bit of skin, they should consider themselves lucky.

Emily looked relieved. "Well, that's good, then. I thought you'd heard about it, and after what happened to your husband, you wouldn't want to come out with us today."

She had been shaken on Saturday night, and for most of yesterday, vowing not to go out in the *Sea Witch* again until it was completely dry from its soaking, but the Maritime Museum's research boat was much bigger, and it would be moored at a protected dive site. There wouldn't be any yahoos speeding through that patch of reef. If they did, they'd end up as another wreck among the historic ones already nestled between the reefs. Besides, she'd be going out in daytime, on a clear day. Drunken Saturday night revellers wouldn't be out menacing the public in the middle of a work day.

And now she knew the boat that had endangered her was stuck in drydock indefinitely, today's trip was looking a whole lot safer.

"I'll have to get back onto a boat sometime. It may as well be now," Anemone said, slinging her bag aboard before climbing over the gunwales herself. "Do I need to get my air tanks out of the car, or will you have enough for me?"

"Jeremy has enough for a small army. Don't worry about bringing your own. We'll have you covered." Emily landed on the deck beside Anemone's bag. "I'll stow this for you."

Anemone stepped into the main cabin, where she found Jeremy. "Emily says you're bringing an army. The brief I got didn't say anything about invading Rottnest."

Jeremy looked puzzled for a moment, then his expression cleared. "Oh, you mean the dive tanks? No, I just wanted to make sure we had enough. We ran out at the Abrolhos, and getting more air out there was a nightmare. Especially when there's only so much good weather for diving out there."

She'd been scheduled to go with them on that trip. Then Morgan had died and she'd transferred. "How did it go? Did you uncover many more secrets? The Great Cameo, maybe?"

Jeremy shook his head. "Just the bodies we knew were under the fishing shacks. They're all gone now. Nothing but ghosts remain."

Anemone nodded. She'd heard the stories — most people who visited Beacon Island preferred to sleep aboard their boats, rather than stay on the island itself after dark. It wasn't called the island of angry ghosts for nothing. "And anything else you found is waiting on the conservation team to see what you have before you report on it?"

"We could do with your expertise. We'd take you back in a heartbeat, you know, even if your secondment isn't over. I'm sure we could find someone else to fill the spot at the prison…"

Anemone closed her eyes. She fitted in among the museum team as easily as if she'd never left, but it wasn't the people who had driven her away. No, it was the talk of shipwrecks and deaths at sea that drove her to tears, and in the Maritime Archaeology division of the museum, everything was about shipwrecks.

"Let's see how I go today, first," she said firmly.

THIRTY-THREE

Anemone double checked her gear, then checked it again, before she ventured off the boat into the water. Everyone else had already submerged, so she was the last to reach the dive trail. She'd forgotten how peaceful it was beneath the surface. Nothing but bubbles and fish, with the distant boom of waves breaking on the outer reef. Oh, she'd missed this.

She kicked slowly along the dive trail,

pausing to check the plaques. They were in surprisingly good condition, given how eager the coral was to colonise anything that stayed beneath the surface for any length of time. No need for a corrosion expert here.

The wreck was another matter. If she hadn't known it was there, hidden beneath the encroaching coral, she could have swum straight past. But there were still straight edges to be seen among the sea life, even after more than a hundred years. The sort of lines nature didn't produce without human intervention. She paused for a long look, letting the camera mounted on her mask get plenty of footage before she moved on. Today was just a preliminary assessment, to look around and see what they needed to focus their attention on during later dives. So the morning was set aside for the dive trail, and the afternoon was for the likely mooring sites.

The dive team had stopped to watch a seal, but Anemone had too much experience with seals trying to steal her gear to want to join them. Instead, she headed back to the boat.

The others surfaced soon after, and they ate lunch while discussing what they'd seen. One of the guys had spotted a turtle, and they all crowded around the laptop screen to see the footage he'd recorded.

The afternoon westerly was in by the time they were scheduled to do the second dive, and Anemone decided to stay in the cabin and watch the live feed instead of joining the divers. It looked like clean, sandy bottom, the perfect place to put in moorings.

The team spread out to identify any potential hazards, and Anemone turned to get changed out of her wetsuit.

"Shit, what's that?" Jeremy said.

"It looks brand new," Emily breathed. "Hey, Anemone, come take a look. How long do you think it could have been down there?"

Anemone answered before she'd even seen the screen. "If there's no coral accretion, less than a year, most likely." She peered at the picture, as the diver circled around the gap in the reef where the fishing boat lay on the section of sandy bottom. Then he dropped lower, and a rock lobster scuttled out of his way.

The registration number came into view. Anemone blinked. That couldn't be right. The *Perfect Catch* hadn't been anywhere near Rottnest. They'd been on the way back from Carnac Island when…

"I need to go down there," she said, zipping up her wetsuit.

Emily and Jeremy were too intent on the screen to hear her. "There's her name – the *Perfect Catch*. It looks like it only sank yesterday. Hey, Anemone, how long do you think…?"

"Eleven months, twenty-three days and about fourteen hours," Anemone said, fighting to keep her voice steady.

Emily laughed. "Wow, that's precise. How can you…"

"That's the boat my husband skippered, on the night he died."

Silence reigned in the cabin.

"I need to go down there. Can you double check my gear for me, please, Jeremy?"

Wordlessly, Jeremy did as she asked, then gave the signal for okay with both hands.

Anemone barely felt the water's chill as it closed over her head. It took her a moment to orient herself, before she saw the fins of the diver who'd been filming the *Catch*.

The current tried to tug her away, but Anemone only kicked harder. She had to see it for herself. To know what had happened…

The ship sat on the bottom, tipped over on an angle like it had been beached on shore. The windows were intact, without even the usual salt crusting. Washed away by the water, Anemone assumed. She switched on her dive torch and shone it through the nearest window. The cabin looked exactly as she remembered it, with the exception of the metal chests stacked up along one wall. One had fallen over on its side, but the impact hadn't been enough to jolt it open.

She moved around to the next window, and

the next. Was that a hint of red?

She swam around to the cabin door and shone her torch through that. Oh, it was red, all right. A big coral trout, printed on the back of the fishing shirt she'd bought Morgan for their last Christmas together.

She reached for the door handle. It moved easily, but tugging the door open was another matter.

In the end, it took two of them to open it halfway, wide enough for Anemone to squeeze inside. She grabbed the shirt, to pull it out from under the console. A small crab scuttled out of the collar, across…across…

White…bone…oh god…

THIRTY-FOUR

"We have to call the police."

"Should we take her to hospital? She hasn't said anything since she surfaced."

"She took all her gear off and put it away perfectly. Maybe she just doesn't want to talk. Would you want to, after finding that? I mean, it looked like one of the *Batavia* bodies. One of the victims."

"Yeah, but you should talk. Especially after

finding something like that."

"Anemone? Are you all right?"

"Fine," she heard herself say. "I just need to get home. Maybe I'm not ready to go out on a boat again yet."

"Mike's pulling everyone out early. The police divers will want to dive the site before we can go any further."

"We'll head back as soon as everyone's aboard. Or we can put you ashore and you can catch a ferry back."

Anemone must have said something, because the next thing she remembered, she was trudging up the stairs to her apartment. Her hand shook, but she managed to get the keys into the lock eventually.

Her bed was waiting with open arms to embrace her, so she flopped down, face first, and welcomed oblivion.

THIRTY-FIVE

She'd gone to bed in daylight, with the blinds wide open, so Dunstan had to wait in the walls until after sunset before he could go to her. At first, she'd just laid there, not moving or saying anything. Then she'd started weeping, and she showed no sign of stopping. His heart ached for her.

The moment the sun slipped below the horizon, he crossed the room in swift strides and slipped in behind her on the bed, drawing her to him. She was sobbing in earnest now, her whole body shaking.

"It's all right. It's all right," he soothed, even though he knew it was a lie. Nothing that could break a woman's heart so thoroughly could ever be in any way right.

"I found him. I found him, Dunstan. Morgan's dead. He really did drown. He went down with his ship and I found him…"

Between sobs, the story spilled out. She'd found her husband's body and the ship he'd been sailing on when he died. She now knew for certain that he was never, ever coming back.

Through it all, every heart-wrenching detail, he held her, until she lay still, and he thought she slept.

Perhaps she did, for a short time.

Darkness had definitely fallen when she spoke again. "I feel so alone, Dunstan."

"You're not alone. You're here with me. I'll keep you safe, I promise."

"What if…what if I want to feel more than just safe?"

He blew out a breath. "Whatever you wish for, name it. If I can give it to you, it is yours."

"I want to feel loved. Like…I'm not alone. I want to feel."

He tightened his arms around her. "I know you can feel this. I'm here, Anemone. I won't leave you."

"I want more than your arms around me. I want to feel you inside me."

It shouldn't have been possible, but his cock stood to attention, like she'd called it by name. The damn thing didn't even have a name.

He couldn't…this was…

"Dunstan, I want you to fuck me."

THIRTY-SIX

Before she could change her mind, Anemone wriggled out of her clothes and threw them on the floor. Then she pressed back against Dunstan, and triumph welled in her breast. She couldn't be imagining it. That had to be his hard length, digging into her hip. He wanted this, too, as much as she did.

She rubbed against him. "Fuck me, Dunstan. Hard. So I forget everything I saw today, and all I can think about is you."

He wrapped his arms around her again, more tentative now he was touching bare skin. Then he slid a hand down her belly, so slowly it was torturous. Finally, he slid one finger inside her.

"More," she demanded, reaching down to make him give it to her.

Something twined around her wrist, holding her fast, before binding her other wrist, too, laying them on the bed beside her. Was that his tail?

Two fingers now, rubbing against her clit on every thrust inside her.

God, this was better than she'd imagined it could be.

Three fingers, one of them hooked at just the right angle to…oh god…

Then his thumb landed on her clit, circling it just right, as his fingers pushed deeper, harder, and she couldn't…couldn't…

She let out a shriek.

"Are you satisfied?" he asked, his voice

rough in her ear.

And that was his…so hard against her hip, even bigger and harder than before.

She should have said yes. One glorious orgasm was more than she deserved. She was a widow. She was supposed to be in mourning, damn it. But she wanted…she wanted…

"I want more," she said. "I want you to fuck me. Properly. Not just with your fingers. Please, Dunstan, I need to feel you inside me."

"Anemone…"

"Don't you dare apologise or tell me you can't. I can feel how hard your cock is, and I want you to fuck me with it. Now." She tried to reach behind her to grab him, but his tail still held her hands fast, so she pressed against him instead, the softness of her body against the hardness of his. "Please!"

His hand moved to her hip, gripping it lightly. The heat of him between her thighs, ready to enter her, but not quite.

"Please, Dunstan!" she begged.

With one powerful thrust, he impaled her,

and she cried out in triumph. She felt that, all right. Couldn't think of anything else but the hard, molten heat of him moving inside her, deeper than she'd imagined possible, filling her…

His hand drifted back to her clit, stroking her to the same beat of his thrusts. Slow and steady, like the heartbeat of the universe. Her universe, for there was nothing else but her and him, and the sensation of what he was doing to her.

She was so lost in the pleasure of his touch, both inside and out, that she barely felt the orgasm building until the feeling was so huge, she was powerless to stop it. It swept her away on a wave of bliss, and all she could do was cry out his name, over and over, because there was space for no one else but Dunstan in her thoughts, while he possessed her body so completely.

THIRTY-SEVEN

Sunlight streamed through Anemone's window when she opened her eyes the next morning. For a moment, she wondered if she'd dreamed it all, but she knew she couldn't have. Between her nakedness, the stone hand cupping her breast and the other stone hand curved around her hip, there was no denying it: Morgan was dead, and she'd just had the best sex of her life with a gargoyle.

She tried to push his hands off her, so she could get up, but they wouldn't move. Instead, she had to wiggle out of his grasp, only to discover that she'd been sharing the bed with an actual statue.

It took her a moment to remember what he'd said about sunlight – how it turned him to stone, like the gargoyle on the roof.

Had she medusaed him, by asking him to go to bed with her? She'd never forgive herself if she had.

She thought for a moment, then grabbed the quilt and flung it over him. Next, she closed the blinds, so sunlight wasn't spilling across the bed any more.

Somewhere in the house, a phone was ringing.

Anemone swore, grabbing a robe to throw around her shoulders as she sprinted toward the sound.

Of course, the call went to voicemail before she found her phone. And it was an unknown number, so she couldn't call them back.

She held the phone in front of her, staring at it, willing them to call back.

Someone began pounding on her front door instead.

She pulled her robe on properly, tied it tightly around her waist, and went to the door. "Who is it?" she called. Only Catena had the keys to the front door, so it had to be...

"It's the police, Dr Seaver. Your neighbour was just leaving for work, so she let us in."

Well, that sucked. No way was she answering the door in just her robe if they were here. "Give me a minute to get dressed, and I'll be right back," she said.

The bed was empty when she reached the bedroom, though the quilt lay in a heap beside the wall, instead of on the bed, where she'd left it. Dunstan must be all right, despite his sunlight exposure, then.

She dressed quickly in the first things she found, then headed back to the front door to let the police in.

"Can we come in?" one of them asked.

She wanted to say no, but she didn't want to talk to them outside on the landing, either. Anemone sighed. "All right."

She led the way to the kitchen. While they said whatever they wanted to say, she could at least make some coffee. Maybe even breakfast.

A chirp drew her attention to the corner, where Lucky sat expectantly beside her empty bowl. Right. The cat needed breakfast, too.

The two officers took seats on the barstools, and then just sat there, silently watching, while Anemone fed the cat and made coffee.

Finally, just to break the silence, she said, "Do you want one?" and pointed at her coffee.

They both shook their heads.

She was quickly losing patience with these two. "Are you here to tell me my husband is dead? Because I already know. First, everyone else got rescued but him. Then, the coroner declared him dead. And yesterday, while I was at work, we found the boat with his body still in it. His skeleton, wearing his shirt, seeing as there wasn't much left of him after almost a year in the water..." Tears filled her eyes, threatening to fall, but she dashed them away. She would not cry in front of these two strangers.

The two men exchanged a look. Finally, one of them said, "I'm Detective Rasul, and this is Detective Nunzio. We're sorry for your loss and sorry to have to bother you at such a difficult time, but we want to know if you recognise this."

He pulled out a tablet, scrolled to something, then held up the screen so she could see it. It was a wall, with red letters scrawled across it in what looked like lipstick:

TELL US WHERE HE IS IF YOU DON'T WANT TO MEET THE SAME FATE

Anemone blinked.

"I don't understand."

Rasul took the tablet back. "Nor does the nurse who bought your old house. She came home from night shift at the hospital and found this."

That's why she didn't recognise it. It was the lounge room wall, which had been covered in bookcases when Anemone and Morgan lived there.

"I still don't understand."

"Somehow the boat you found was leaked to the media. Luckily, we've managed to keep the news about your husband's body and the other items in the boat under wraps for now, but it looks like someone saw the news and came to find you. Or him, if they think he's still alive."

That poor nurse. At least she hadn't been home when they'd come to her house. If they'd come here, Dunstan would have beaten them to a pulp in the name of protecting her. Well, probably, if they hadn't come when they were…busy…

Her mind went back to what the detective had said. "What other items?" She hadn't seen another body, but seeing Morgan's was bad enough. It's not like she'd looked for anyone else…

"What do you know about illegal drugs, Doctor Seaver?"

She blew out a breath. "Um, that they're illegal? Look, I know I have a background in chemistry, which means everyone thinks I'm just one bad decision away from *Breaking Bad*, but my PhD was in marine corrosion, and my job is conservation of artefacts for a museum where I'm one of the assistant curators. The only thing I know about illegal drugs is that they're bad."

"Did you know that your husband was involved in the illegal drug trade?"

Anemone burst out laughing. "Morgan? You can't be serious. He wouldn't even take paracetamol for a headache, he was so anti drugs. I mean, his mum died of an accidental drug overdose. And no, they weren't illegal drugs. She and Morgan's dad were in a car accident, and she had some prescription pain medication, which she accidentally overdosed on. Morgan's dad found her and…well, I imagine you know he felt responsible for the accident, and her death, and he didn't want to live without her, and there was still enough of her pain medication left..." Anemone swallowed. "Morgan was devastated. That's why he wouldn't take anything, just in case. So there is absolutely no way he would have anything to do with drugs, legal or illegal."

Another exchanged glance. "Then can you explain this?" Another swipe of the tablet, and a new picture on the screen. This time, it showed a bunch of metal boxes, sitting open on a table.

"Those boxes were in the boat cabin with Morgan's body," Anemone said slowly. "But there's no way he would have agreed to transport drugs. He was covering for Janus Smith, the owner of the *Perfect Catch*, who was sick and couldn't take the charter, so he asked Morgan to do it for him. If Morgan had known there were drugs in those boxes...he never would have boarded that boat."

"It's methamphetamine. The street value of a haul this big is more than ten times what the boat was worth, or at least what the insurance payout was."

Anemone shrugged. "I wouldn't know anything about that. It wasn't Morgan's boat, or mine. If it was insured, that was Janus's business, not ours."

"Doctor Seaver, did your husband have enemies?"

"No! He was a lovely, kind man, willing to do anyone a favour, up to and including sailing Janus's rust bucket of a charter boat for him when the man was too stingy to hire staff to cover for him. I can't think of anyone who didn't like Morgan. He was…wonderful." Now she was tearing up again, and she couldn't stop it this time. Crying into her coffee, no less.

"Doctor Seaver, did you get a close look at the body?"

Anemone closed her eyes. She had video footage of the dive, but she didn't need to download a single second of it, when the whole thing played on repeat in the back of her mind. "It was face down, wearing the shirt I bought him, on the floor under the console. When I tried to pull it out, his head sort of...fell to pieces..." Just like the *Batavia* bodies. Bludgeoned to death by their own shipmates...

The detectives were nodding, like this was a good thing. "A skull fracture, likely the cause of death, though it's impossible to be certain, after this long in the water."

Someone hit him. Someone hit him on the back of the head when he found out about the drugs, and objected, or threatened to call the police. Because Morgan would never stay quiet.

And if the drug dealers believed he was still alive, and knew where their missing drugs were...no wonder they were looking for him.

But at their old address, which they'd left a year ago, to move here.

It was only a matter of time before they discovered their mistake, and came after her. Or worse, hurt that poor nurse who had nothing to do with any of this.

"Doctor Seaver…"

She gripped the bench, in an effort to stop herself from swaying. This was too much, first thing in the morning, before she'd even finished her first cup of coffee. Especially after everything that had happened yesterday.

"Doctor Seaver, here's my card. If you think of anything important, about your husband, or the boat, or what you saw in the boat yesterday, please give us a call. And please don't leave town, just in case we have more questions."

They rose to go.

Hysterical laughter bubbled up. "Where would I go? All the borders are shut to contain this stupid virus. Even if I wanted to, my life, my home, even my husband's body, everything is here. If you find out anything about the people who killed my husband, you'll find me here."

"We're very sorry for your loss, Doctor Seaver. We'll see ourselves out."

Actually, she saw them out, and once she'd

shut the door firmly behind them, she bolted it, too. Couldn't be too careful, with killer drug dealers about.

THIRTY-EIGHT

A message from Emily told her they wouldn't be diving until the police were done raising the boat, so she wouldn't be needed today. Anemone considered calling in sick to work, but she couldn't stand sitting around at home with her thoughts in such a tangled mess, so she changed into some work clothes, and went into the prison.

Beth was delighted to see her, and

immediately set her to cataloguing the artefacts the archaeologists had brought in on Friday. It was mind-numbingly repetitive enough not to require too much thought, while at the same time requiring sufficient focus to keep her mind from wandering to other things she'd rather avoid thinking about. Boats and bodies, for a start.

The sun was slipping down behind approaching stormclouds as Anemone walked home, giving her just enough time to heat something up for dinner before Dunstan appeared, looking as alive as ever, and as if he hadn't turned into a statue in her bed that morning.

He looked like the hot man who had made love to her last night. If she closed her eyes, she could still feel him…

But she couldn't think about that now. She needed to tell him about Morgan's murder, and the other things the police had shared.

In between bites of green curry and rice (made in the slow cooker on Sunday), she told him everything. By the time she was done, there was nothing but a few grains of rice stuck to the side of her bowl, and the bottle of wine she'd opened to have with it was half gone.

"The only thing I know for sure is that Morgan never would have had anything to do with drug smuggling. So if someone killed him, it was because of that."

Unlike the police, Dunstan just nodded. At least he believed her.

"It sounds to me that the people with answers were the smugglers who were on the boat with him. The ones who were rescued. And perhaps the owner of the boat, for he was the one who was hired to transport the drugs in the first place," Dunstan said.

Anemone spread her arms wide. "But what can I do about that? The police are probably already talking to them, or they will soon, and whoever wrote that threat on the wall meant it for me. I'm hardly going to go to them and make it easy for them. I mean, if they killed

Morgan, there's nothing to stop them from doing the same to me…especially if they want the drugs, which the police already have."

"You don't have to do anything. Now, first things first…you're assuming it's murder, but what if they didn't mean to kill him? Especially if they think he's still alive. Maybe they got into a fight, and one of them got in a good punch that knocked him down and he hit his head when he fell. He might have even stood up, and seemed fine. I've seen it before, men brawling and then walking back to their lodgings, only to be found dead in their beds in the morning. Maybe his death was an accident."

Anemone swallowed. "Manslaughter, not murder, but that doesn't make it right. Morgan shouldn't have died."

Dunstan inclined his head. "Agreed. Perhaps his shipmates brought the contraband aboard without telling him what he was carrying. Maybe no one knew but the man whose boxes they were, and your husband stumbled across them." He flipped his hand over. "Or…perhaps they all knew. His shipmates, the owner, everyone except your husband."

Anemone nodded slowly.

"Which means, the best person to ask is the owner of the boat."

Anemone started to laugh. "You don't know Janus. He's as slippery as a bucket of eels, and greedy to boot. He begged to have his boat included in my PhD project, just so he could get a free anti-corrosion paint job on his rust bucket, and then when I saw it and chose his boat as my control, the one without any coating, seeing as it was so long overdue a new coating that it might as well not have any, he pitched an absolute fit. He's hated me ever since. Funny, seeing as I got along with his wife, Lucy, really well, but I haven't seen her since they got divorced."

"How much would it cost to charter his boat for a night, like those smugglers did?"

Anemone shrugged. She'd never needed a

charter, what with the Sea Witch and all. Even if she had, everyone at the yacht club had owed Morgan a favour for something, so she'd only have had to ask…

"You probably won't need to charter the whole boat. Janus runs night fishing charters, which are only a couple hundred dollars per person. If you joined one of those, you wouldn't have to charter the whole boat."

Dunstan looked horrified. "Two hundred dollars for a night's sail?"

Ah. Inflation had changed prices a lot since Dunstan was a boy. "I'm sure I owe you that much and more for fixing my ceiling. I'll get some cash out in the morning, and find out when the next charter's running. Just…please be careful, okay?"

Dunstan grinned. "You needn't worry about me. If he tries to punch me, it's his hand that will break, not my head, I promise you. And if I throw a few punches of my own…" He looked positively gleeful at the prospect.

Anemone only felt sick. "Please, don't.

There's been enough violence. I don't want anyone else hurt. I just want to know that whoever killed Morgan goes to prison, hopefully for a long time, and that they won't come after me, or anyone else."

He bowed his head. "Don't you worry. I'm your sworn protector, and I will do whatever is necessary to keep you safe."

And that worried her more than ever.

THIRTY-NINE

Dunstan had barely been aboard the *Catch of the Day* for five minutes, and he already knew the captain, Janus Smith, was more in love with money than anything else in the world, even his boat. The other men aboard didn't seem to notice the dents and rust stains marking the gunwales, or perhaps it was so dark they couldn't see them.

But they handed over their money readily

enough. When they held out a plastic card to the beeping machine in Janus's hands, he frowned, but when they produced cash, his grin got just a little bit wider. Dunstan was loath to hand so much money to the man, but this was necessary to avenge Anemone's husband…and keep her safe, he told himself as he forced himself to part with the fortune Anemone had given him.

Janus just accepted it with a nod and pocketed the notes, as if he did this every day. Perhaps he did, and the battered boat belied how wealthy the man was. But if he'd made that wealth at the cost of Anemone's husband's life…

Dunstan clenched his fists. If his suspicions proved true, he'd destroy this boat just as he'd done to the wankers' vessel. He made a mental note to ask Anemone what wankers were.

"Sit down, grab a beer, and make yourself comfortable. We'll be heading out to one of my favourite secret fishing spots, before we drop a few lines and see what we catch. Then we'll move onto another spot, and maybe even a third before the night is out. We'll do some high speed trolling travelling between spots, and see if we can hook a wahoo or two along the way, too." Janus flipped open a blue chest, filled with ice and cans, and began tossing cans to the half a dozen men assembled on his deck.

The others opened their drinks, but Dunstan didn't bother. It wasn't like he'd be drinking it, anyway. Instead, he pretended to swig from the closed can, laughing at the other men's jokes, even if he didn't understand half of them.

Finally, they dropped anchor, and Janus moved around the deck, offering tips to the men as they plied the waves with their fishing rods in search of fish.

Dunstan caught a few fish while he waited, cutting their throats and tossing them into the box Janus had indicated was to hold their catch, until finally Janus came to him.

"Have you caught anything yet?" Janus

asked, examining Dunstan's tackle.

Dunstan shrugged. "Three so far. I'm not really interested in fishing, so much as going for a night sail. I don't have as much time to go out, like I used to, what with my roster and all." He and Anemone had devised a cover story for him, which he'd dutifully memorised, even if he found it hard to believe. "This time when I came home, I found my woman had kicked me out. Shacked up with someone else. So I'm kind of at a loose end until I find someplace new to stay, or until my next rotation starts."

Janus nodded. "FIFO, are you? Yeah, that's hard. I mean, working away all hours of the day, and doing what's best for your family, only to have the bitch turn on you when you get home? I know what it's like. I used to do a bunch of week-long charters for mining guys, just like you, and then one day, she up and left me. She swears there isn't another man, but there has to be, you know? She hasn't worked a day in her life since the first kid was born, and there's three of them. Someone's got to pay for their school fees and things. And that Family Court, bunch of criminals pretending to be lawyers, if you ask me. They cleaned me out and almost took my boat. Gave it all to her – the money I earned, working my arse off, while she was sitting on her arse all day, watching cartoons with the kids." Janus shook his head.

In what world were women suddenly reviled for taking care of their children? Dunstan desperately wanted to ask the man more, but he didn't dare. Anemone would explain it to him later, he hoped.

"Now she expects me to babysit the kids on weekends – even got the court to write it into the divorce agreement! – so she can cheat on me with the mystery guy she keeps saying she isn't sleeping with. I told her I can't have them in the evenings, because I work nights, doing night fishing and all, but that didn't stop her. She drops them off in the morning, and picks them up at night. I sleep through most of it, except when the kids play too loud. Then I shout at 'em until they pipe down. I don't know what she was whining about, taking care of kids isn't hard. As if sitting around on her arse, watching them and doing nothing, isn't how her arse got so big." Janus tapped his nose. "You know what, though? I fixed her. The court said I have to give her part of what I earn, to support her and the kids, as if we were still married, but that's why I do so many night charters. You see, when you pay cash, I can keep it off the books, and if it's not on the books, then I don't owe her nothing."

Dunstan felt sick, which was quite a feat for a gargoyle who wasn't sure he even had a stomach, let alone anything in it to throw up. This excuse for a man wanted to desert his wife and children, instead of supporting them, like any honourable man would do. He wanted to punch the man, but for Anemone's sake, he couldn't.

He forced himself to nod instead. "That's clever. My girl said she was pregnant, and we were going to get married, then when I got back…she's married to some other guy and telling him the baby's his!"

Janus just shook his head. "Bitch. If the other idiot believes that lying, cheating whore, without a DNA test, then he deserves her. You're better off without her, mate. Here, tell you what. Any time you want to come back on a night fishing trip, and you pay cash, I'll give you a ten percent discount."

The perfect opening for what he needed to ask. "What if I come every night, until I go back to site? Then I don't need to find a place to stay yet."

Janus frowned. "Well, I do charters like this most nights, but occasionally I do a private one. Like a bachelor party. I couldn't take you out on those nights."

"What if you told them I was your deckhand?" Dunstan asked eagerly. "I'd still pay you the same. They'd never need to know."

He could see the wheels turning in the

man's brain. Extra money and a free pair of hands to help him? The greedy bastard couldn't possibly turn it down.

"All right," Janus said slowly. "But you'll have to show me you know your way around a boat before that. So you can pass as a deckhand."

Dunstan nodded eagerly, promising to be a fast learner who'd do everything that was asked of him. Well, until he didn't, of course, but Janus didn't need to know that.

They returned to the harbour as the first streaks of dawn were colouring the sky.

Dunstan raced home to give Anemone the good news.

FORTY

Anemone couldn't sleep. Between the nightmares of Morgan's body, or herself lost at sea, or waking up in a panic because she thought she'd heard a noise that was either Lucky or the house settling…if Dunstan had been home, she might have persuaded him to give her another glorious night of distraction, but he was off fishing for information with Janus.

The sun wasn't even up when she finally gave in and decided to go into work early. It wasn't like she could sleep anyway.

But as she stepped out of the front door, she noticed the café across the road was lit up, with the doors wide open and the most amazing smell wafting all the way over to her nose.

Coffee and a muffin.

She was inside before she'd even decided she wanted them. But when she saw the tray of muffins, she wanted them all.

"Good morning!" the woman behind the counter said.

Anemone couldn't seem to drag her eyes away from the muffins. "One of…all of them, please. And a coffee. Flat white today, a big one." She looked up to meet the woman's eyes, and recognised her. "Oh, Tacey, right?"

Tacey grinned. "Yep. And I should probably ask for your name, not just so I can call you when your coffee's ready, but so I don't call you Muffin Addict in my head."

"When the muffins are as good as yours, addiction's inevitable," Anemone said. "But my name is Anemone."

"Like the coral?"

That's what Morgan had said when they first met. A twinge of sadness plucked at her heart, but she pushed it away. "Yeah, like the coral. Or the flowers. My mother thought they were really pretty, until she discovered the flowers are poisonous. The sea creature isn't any nicer, though – it's venomous, related to jellyfish." That made her sound horrible. For the first time, Anemone wondered if her mother hadn't liked her much.

Tacey only looked intrigued. "So are you more like the flower, or the coral? Don't bite me or I'll kill you, or come closer so I can eat you!"

Anemone hesitated. Neither sounded like her. "Well, I'm not really into biting…"

Tacey nodded. "Coral, then. You can look, but you can't touch."

Unless you had skin made of living stone,

like Dunstan. Anemone sighed. She'd see him tonight, after the sun went down. Then he could tell her all about his fishing trip.

"Oh, and speaking of looking…we have an artist in residence in the evenings now. He's quite talented. You should come in and have your portrait drawn, all while drinking your coffee. Or eating your muffin. Or both!"

Anemone laughed, and said she'd think about it. Maybe one evening when Dunstan was out, and she had nothing better to do. Or she could bring Lucky, and ask him to draw the cat for her.

She should probably contact the shelter, to say that Lucky had settled down into a proper house cat now, and she was ready for adoption.

A lump welled up in her throat at the thought. She didn't want to lose Lucky. What if…she contacted the shelter, and said she wanted to adopt her, not just foster her? After all, she'd already named her, and Lucky was happily settled in her apartment. Better yet, she'd bonded with Dunstan, and she'd seen him patting the cat on occasion, so the feeling was evidently mutual.

Picking up her coffee and bag of muffins, Anemone thanked Tacey again and headed off to work.

FORTY-ONE

"He doesn't deserve to be a father, treating his children and their mother like that," Dunstan finished.

Anemone regarded him thoughtfully, like she was still mulling over all the things he'd told her. "And yet we're still giving him money, feeding his greed. It could just be a bachelor party, like he said, not a smuggling trip at all. People charter boats a lot, and a fishing trip with the boys is just such a normal thing to do, nobody would even think twice about it."

"I wasn't certain about it at first, either, but the more he talked about it…I mean, it started out as just a private charter, with no other guests allowed, and then he started saying things about how they go right offshore for this one, so there's a better chance of catching the best fish. He'd had a lot of beer by then, so maybe I didn't hear properly, but he said there's more profit out the back of Rottnest than there ever was at any of his inshore fishing spots. I don't know what it's like now, but in my day, smuggling paid far better than fishing, as long as you didn't get caught. If you did get caught, you'd be hanged."

Anemone shuddered. "Barbaric times. Thank goodness things have changed. Now smugglers just go to prison, like all the other criminals. Nothing so cruel as hanging or hard labour or…did you know there were regular floggings at the prison? One of the jewels of the museum's collection is the original jarrah whipping post they used to tie the prisoners to before they beat them. Men…and sometimes even children!"

Times truly had changed if such things no longer happened. Dunstan remembered the bite of the lash, but he didn't dare tell her. Best she not know that his own sweat and blood had soaked into the whipping post she reviled.

"Well, I'll go along with this private charter, to see if I'm right or not. Best case scenario, I get to see the smugglers in action, and we can come up with a plan to rat them out."

Anemone still didn't seem happy. "All right."

FORTY-TWO

After a week of anxiety about Dunstan going out on a boat trip that could be a drug delivery, Anemone was ready to kiss him when he came home.

Except…the news wasn't good. After Janus had cruised past Rottnest, he'd met up with another boat. They'd transferred a number of boxes, just like the ones the police had found with Morgan's body, from the other boat to the *Catch of the Day*, before sailing back to Fremantle just before dawn.

They needed a plan, and Dunstan's first idea – to sink both of these boats with everyone aboard, just like they'd done to Morgan – wasn't something Anemone could allow.

"Capital punishment isn't done these days. People pay for their crimes, they don't die for them. The police need to catch them, with enough evidence to convict them. You can't just kill them," Anemone tried to explain, but Dunstan was having none of it.

"I don't understand. How do you expect me to contact the police from way offshore, and make sure the boats are still there when they arrive?" he persisted. "They're boats, they move. I mean, if it was a sailing boat, I could leave it dead in the water in a number of ways. If I broke the mast, they couldn't sail anywhere. If I snapped the rudder, or broke off the wheel, they couldn't steer, but with these motor boats, not to mention life rafts and tenders, I wouldn't have the first idea how to stop them. I don't even know how the motor works."

Anemone nodded. "Wait…did you say taking the wheel off? That's what some of the yacht club members do when they sail to other marinas, to stop theft. Of course, all a thief would have to do is carry a spare wheel and they could steal whatever they wanted to, but if they were thirty kilometres or more offshore, a spare wheel would be much harder to find…"

Dunstan nodded. That he could do. "But what about the police? How would they find them?"

Anemone considered. Usually, she'd say radio, because every sailor she knew could manage the basics on a radio, but Dunstan was from a time before radio existed. Not to mention if anyone recorded his distress call, they'd have his voiceprint to compare to him later. For this to work, Dunstan had to be a ghost, someone who didn't exist. The easiest way to send a distress call from that far offshore was an EPIRB, but they had to be registered, which meant tying it back to her, if not Dunstan. That would never do.

Morgan had always kept a couple handy, just in case, even though they rarely went far enough offshore to need one. In fact, she'd seen them on the *Sea Witch*, and made a mental note to have them checked and re-registered, seeing as they were coming up on the two year mark for that soon.

But until she did…the beacons they had were both registered in Morgan's name. And what better ghost than an actual dead man?

"I might know a way," she said slowly. "It's called an EPIRB. Emergency position indicating radio beacon. They activate when they get wet, or you can flip a switch to activate them manually. I'll get one from the *Sea Witch* and show you…"

By the time Anemone went to bed, she and Dunstan had a plan they both believed could work. Maybe. With a lot of luck and maybe a miracle.

That didn't stop her from worrying about

what might go wrong, though.

FORTY-THREE

Dunstan couldn't believe his luck. Everything had gone exactly as Anemone had planned. With the swell rougher than the week before, they'd lashed both boats together to pass the boxes over the gunwales, carrying them down into the hold, where Dunstan had been waiting to take each of the smugglers down, one by one. Then he'd locked them in the hold.

When the last box was aboard the *Catch of*

the Day, he'd knocked Janus out and locked him in the privy, before heading over to the other vessel to do the same to their crew. Three half-starved fishermen were no match for one gargoyle, and he soon had them lying on the floor of the hold, locked in with their stinking catch.

That done, he'd hopped overboard to wind the anchor chains together, so even if they managed to escape and untie the ropes, they'd never manage to untangle the anchors, short of cutting them off entirely. Both wheels he tossed overboard as he headed back to Janus.

Dunstan knew what Anemone had said about not wanting violence, but what she didn't know wouldn't hurt her. Besides, she deserved answers about how her husband had died.

So he tied Janus to the ladder that led up to the fly bridge, then threw a bucket of sea water over him to rouse him. The man came up spluttering.

"What...what are you?"

Dunstan grinned. Instead of human FIFO worker John Stan, he'd decided to confront the smuggler in all his gargoyle glory. Wings, horns and all.

"Are you a demon? Am I in hell?"

Dunstan just grinned wider.

"I didn't do anything! I'm just the driver! I drive the boat, and take the goods in to shore. I have nothing to do with what happens to them after I land them."

He tossed his head wildly. "Where's John? What did you do with John? He's a passenger, his name's on the books, I'll get in trouble if he doesn't make it back."

"Like Morgan Seaver didn't make it back?"

Janus shook his head. "I had nothing to do with that. I had gastro, okay? I couldn't skipper a boat when I couldn't even stand up. He was supposed to take them out, and then come straight back. That was it. It's not my fault he tried to call the courier boat in when he saw it. They took him out before he could report what he thought was a foreign fishing vessel.

He never even saw the cargo, when it was transferred. But the passengers…none of them could drive the boat, and when they hit a reef on the way back, they had to take to the tender to escape, before it sank. It wasn't until later they realised they were missing Morgan. When the tender ran out of fuel, halfway back to Fremantle, they jumped ship and sank that, and told the rescue crew a story about how they'd been fishing off Carnac Island, so they wouldn't find the boat or the body. Or the cargo. Only when they tried to go back to find it themselves, they couldn't…"

He continued in this vein for some time. When Dunstan was certain Janus didn't have any new information to add, he knocked the man out again, and threw him in the hold with the other smugglers.

One last thing to do, and he could go home to Anemone.

He dug out the beacon Anemone had given him, and stuck it to the front of the boat, just above the water line. Then he ripped off the top and switched it on. A little red blinking light told him he'd activated it, just like Anemone had said.

Mission accomplished, Dunstan flapped his wings and commenced his flight home.

FORTY-FOUR

When the sun rose, Dunstan hadn't returned. Anemone knew that didn't mean something bad had happened, but she couldn't seem to silence the thought that this was how she'd lost Morgan.

While her coffee brewed, she picked up her phone to skim the morning news. There was a brief article saying that someone had set off an emergency beacon near Rottnest, and that marine rescue crews were investigating, before the article ended with the distinctly unsatisfying promise that there was more to come.

At work, everyone seemed to be exchanging glances with each other and not looking at her. Anemone let it go on for an hour before she finally snapped. "What is it? What's the bad news everyone else has heard except me?"

Luke, who looked like he'd had less sleep than Anemone last night, piped up, "It's probably nothing, but there was a boat in trouble on the morning news."

"Oh, is that all? Yeah, I heard about that."

Beth laid her hand on Anemone's arm, her eyes brimming with sympathy. "No one wanted to say anything in front of you because…well, your husband…and today of all days…"

Today? Anemone checked the date. A year ago to the day, she'd lost Morgan. And their baby. No wonder she was worried about Dunstan. She'd be worried about her worst enemy, if they were out on a boat today.

She swallowed. "Every time I hear about a boat in trouble, my heart skips a beat. It probably always will. I just…send a hope out into the universe, that all will be well, that no one else will lose someone like I did, and then…well, I guess I find something else to occupy my attention. Speaking of which, does anyone have something that will distract me for the day? Bonus points if you can keep me away from my computer so I'm not checking the news every five minutes."

Luke came to her rescue – the cell with the last remaining original 1850s wash basin was due for conservation works. The basin itself wasn't the issue, but they'd found mould in the cell, which was a danger not just to the plumbing but the limestone cell walls and the jarrah flooring, so if she could put on a protective suit and take a closer look, before putting together a brief to go to tender for conservation works…

Any other day, Anemone would have

laughed in his face for suggesting she do something so menial, but right now, inspecting the plumbing sounded perfect.

By the time she headed home, she'd rediscovered her loathing for hazmat suits, sworn roundly at the vagueness of all the previous tender documentation, and cobbled together a draft of what sort of cleaning should happen to that cell, if the budget stretched to proper conservation work and not just the sort of patch job that had been done every other time.

But as she walked home, she sent out more than a hope to the universe. This time, it was a siren call that the universe would return Dunstan to her, a year to the day since she lost her husband. Surely no one could be so unlucky twice in one lifetime.

FORTY-FIVE

Dunstan had never flown so far in his life. There was water below him, clearly visible as the sun threatened to crest over the horizon, and miles of ocean still separated him from Fremantle. He wouldn't be home this morning, and he couldn't fly any further, either. The moment the sun rose, he'd become a statue and fall right out of the sky, into the waves below.

Cursing, he folded his wings, and dropped into the sea.

Down, down he fell, until he reached the sea floor, where no light could touch him. Not a moment too soon, either, for he had to shake the stone stiffness from his limbs for several minutes before he could resume his journey home. One step after the other, along the sea floor. Good thing gargoyles didn't need to breathe.

FORTY-SIX

The moment she entered her apartment, Anemone called his name. But only Lucky answered the call, chirping for her dinner. She fed the cat, but there was no sign of Dunstan.

The sunset blazed through the eastern windows, a blur of orange she could barely see through her tears. She couldn't lose Dunstan. She wouldn't. She'd go down to the harbour and wait for him, as soon as it was dark.

But what if he came here instead, while she was down there?

But…but…

She raced up to the roof, peering out in all directions in the hope that she'd see him coming. Walking along the road. Flying through the sky. Something. But he wasn't there.

She would go to the harbour, she decided. Down the stairs, out the front door to the landing, then down the staircase to the foyer…

"Anemone?"

"Dunstan?"

She flew into his arms, kissing him for all she was worth. She wrapped her arms and legs around him, not caring that her skirt rode up to her waist. All she cared about was that he was here, safe, with her, and he was…

"Why are you naked?"

He chuckled. "Clothes weighed me down in the water. Then I had to wait until dark to fly back, so no one would see me. But I'm here now."

"Yes, oh yes."

He was so hot and hard between her legs. Why was she still wearing underwear? She needed to feel him inside her. Now.

"Dunstan, please," she moaned.

He slid two fingers between her skin and those stupid knickers, and tore them away. Now there was nothing between them.

"Fuck me. Please."

He slammed her back against the wall, entering her with a fierceness that matched her own need for him.

"Yes, yes, oh, yes…"

Hard and fast, like nothing she'd ever known before. Better than any time before. She could barely believe it, but she was about to come already.

She buried her face in his shoulder, certain she was going to scream.

"Did you just bite me?" He laughed. "I don't think a woman's ever bitten me before. I might need to bite you back for that. But where…"

His hands made quick work of her shirt

buttons and her bra, baring her breasts.

She arched her back, begging him to do whatever he wished to her.

"Anemone? Anemone!"

That wasn't his voice. It sounded like Catena, in a panic as she pounded on Anemone's front door on the landing above.

Anemone blinked. She and Dunstan were in the foyer, backed into the little alcove beneath the stairs. His wings held her up while he was still buried balls-deep inside her, as his hands cupped her breasts, his mouth inches away from ravaging her in the most delightful way possible.

"She's not home." That was a male voice, also upstairs. "What did you intend to tell her, anyway? That there's a thing in her dungeon, a winged, horned demon who means to seduce her so he can have his wicked way with her? She'll never believe you."

"I have to try. Anemone!" Catena pounded on the door again.

Anemone's eyes met Dunstan's. He gave her

a lazy grin, curling his tail around her nipple and giving it a squeeze. She gasped, then clapped her hand over her mouth, hoping they hadn't heard.

He began to move inside her again, exquisitely slow and oh so deep. She forgot all about the neighbours and dungeons and demons, horned or otherwise, and lost herself to sensation as Dunstan took first one nipple into his mouth, then the other.

She was close, so close, when he stilled and said, "I think they've gone. It's safe to go upstairs."

She didn't want to stop. She wanted him to finish…finish what he was doing to her, or she was definitely going to bite him this time.

"Unless you want to send your big, winged, horned demon thing back to the dungeon. I'd prefer to take you up to your bed, where I can have my wicked way with you, over and over again." His eyes dared her to protest.

"Upstairs. Now," she managed to say.

His wings wrapped around her, and she only

had a moment to take a breath before she was whirled through walls to her bedroom.

He was still inside her. And she was so, so close…

"Sit on the bed," she commanded.

He did, settling her in his lap. Anemone rose up onto her knees, then sank down on him again. She grasped his horns in her hands. "We're doing things my wicked way first," she said.

FORTY-SEVEN

Several hours and countless orgasms later, Anemone lay beside Dunstan on the bed, breathless and aching, but happier than she could remember since...since...a year ago.

"Why would my neighbour try to warn me about you?" she asked. "How would she even know about you?"

Dunstan shrugged. "Perhaps she saw me, on my way back from the harbour. I succeeded, by the way. The plan went exactly the way it was supposed to. I could see the beacon blinking as I flew away."

Anemone felt her cheeks grow hot. She'd been so worried about Dunstan, then so happy to see him back safe, that she hadn't cared about her husband's killers any more. All she'd wanted to do was make love with her monster. Up against the wall, on the bed, bent over the blanket box, then back on the bed…

She was fast becoming addicted to his cock, if she wasn't already. And his mouth, and his wings, and his hands, and that troublesome tail…if she didn't know better, she'd think she was in love with him.

And the thought of losing him…

Who was she kidding? She was in love with him.

She traced a line down his rock hard abdominal muscles, stopping just short of his ever-hard cock. One of the perks of being made of living stone, he'd said.

"We should make love to celebrate your

victory," she said.

"Or I could finally have my wicked way with you, like your neighbours warned you about." He sat up, then patted his thigh. "Come sit in my lap, sweet lass."

She'd barely sat down, when his wings curled around her, holding her in place.

"Hold onto my horns," he whispered. "So I can take you on the ride of your life."

Which he did.

FORTY-EIGHT

It was a week before the police arrived at her door again. A week of busy days at work, and heavenly nights in bed with Dunstan. Not even on her honeymoon had she had this much sex, but the moment the sun went down and he appeared, she was desperate for more.

But in the afternoon light, with Detectives Nunzio and Rasul on her doorstep, she shoved away any thoughts of sex and tried to look like

Morgan's grieving widow, for surely it was his murder they were here to discuss.

She let them sit in her kitchen again, but she didn't make coffee this time. She'd already had enough for any normal Saturday, and she intended to buy her next one from the Shut Up Café across the road before they closed for the day.

"The coroner is finished with your husband's remains, and is ready to release them to you so you can lay them to rest," Detective Rasul began.

Anemone nodded. They'd already had a funeral service for Morgan, even though there'd been no body in the casket. Now there was a body, she'd have to arrange for him to be cremated. He'd always said he wanted his ashes scattered at sea, and she would give him that. "Thank you."

"Doctor Seaver, what do you know about Janus Smith?"

She blinked. "He owned the boat my husband was aboard when he died. The *Perfect*

Catch."

"Yes, but what did you know about him?"

She blew out a breath. "I knew him as my friend Lucy's husband. A member of the yacht club with a beaten up charter boat he didn't take proper care of. He was friends with Morgan…everyone was friends with Morgan, that's just how he was…but I didn't like him. He was sleazy, especially when Lucy wasn't around. After they got divorced, I avoided him altogether."

The two men nodded. Nunzio still took notes, but Rasul had set his tablet down, eager to ask the next question.

"Do you know why Mr Smith would have one of your husband's emergency beacons on his boat?"

Anemone shrugged. "Well, Morgan did take the *Perfect Catch* out that fateful night. He never went out without an EPIRB, so I'm sure he had one with him. Which is weird, come to think of it, because why didn't it go off when the boat sank? I thought they activated when they got wet. Or was the boat too deep for the beacon to get picked up by satellite before the signal died?"

The two men exchanged glances. Whatever it was, neither of them wanted to be the one to tell her.

"A beacon registered to your husband activated a week ago, about forty kilometres offshore. We found it attached to Mr Smith's new boat, the *Catch of the Day*, which was tangled up with another boat, a foreign fishing vessel, with a very interesting cargo."

Dunstan hadn't mentioned any cargo, or anything about the other boat, so Anemone didn't have to feign her surprise. "What was it?"

"Well, drugs, but also a large quantity of trepang. Several species of sea cucumber found only in protected marine parks along the West Australian coast."

Her breath hissed out. "Illegal fishing and drug smuggling? I hope those men go to jail for a long time. That's horrible."

"Is there anything else you can tell us about Janus Smith?"

Anemone shook her head. "Nothing I haven't already told you. I barely knew the man."

"What about his new deckhand, John Stan?"

"Who?" She tried to make her face as blank as possible.

"Mr Smith has a new deckhand, a man he was training to help him in his charter business, by the name of John Stan. They hadn't signed any new contracts yet, so all we have is his word that this man exists and the testimony of one of the passengers, a rather cooperative man who deeply regrets punching your husband…"

Morgan's killer. Anemone swallowed. "You're saying this man, John Stan, is responsible for my husband's death?"

"No, no, he's just a person of interest. One of Mr Smith's passengers last week, when the beacon was activated, confessed to being on board the *Perfect Catch* the night your husband died. And both he and Mr Smith have the most remarkable story, about a deckhand who disappeared and a demon who attacked their boat. Mr Smith said the demon tied him up and did things to him."

"A demon." Well, Dunstan was a bit of a sex fiend, but she was no worse than him, and she was definitely human. "Are you sure they didn't see the Moth Man? There have been some videos on the internet...or aliens. I've heard aliens are into kinky things like that."

Nunzio shook his head. "I don't know what they saw. Maybe they were all drunk, or they made it up. We will get the real story in time, and I strongly encourage you to tell us all you know now, or we'll have to return to ask more questions."

Anemone shrugged again. "No one wants to get to the bottom of my husband's death more than I do, detectives. If you have questions, I'm happy to answer them. But if you're looking for imaginary monsters, you won't find them here. I'm a scientist. I believe in what I can observe, not some hoax someone made up. If you had a picture of this deckhand, or the demon..."

Rasul offered her a smile. "Much like the legal system, Doctor Seaver. We believe in evidence, and what it can prove. Unreliable testimony about demons and men who don't seem to exist...well, it does seem far-fetched. Of course no one thought to take a picture, even though the men all had their phones with them. Perhaps they intend to plead insanity for their crimes in court."

"I don't know much about court cases, criminal or otherwise. But I do wish you luck with your investigation," Anemone said. "Did your informant have anything useful for you that does help?"

Aside from his wild stories about demons and deckhands, he'd told them everything he knew about the drug trade as he knew it, including the people who'd daubed threatening messages on that nurse's wall, so it sounded like there were a lot more arrests to come.

Anemone, and the nurse, would be safe.

It took another minute or two of small talk before she could close the door firmly behind them. Anemone checked her watch. She still had time to get coffee and a muffin.

FORTY-NINE

Anemone stared at the muffin cabinet, not quite able to come to terms with the emptiness. She'd decided in the short walk across the road that she deserved an extra muffin after that interrogation, and now she couldn't even have one.

Rochelle offered a sympathetic smile. "I'm sorry, we're out of muffins today. But we do have some new white chocolate and raspberry mousse cheesecakes. Individual ones. Layers of white chocolate mousse over raspberry mouse, on a dark chocolate biscuit base." She pointed at the cabinet. "It goes really well with a Vienna dark hot chocolate."

Anemone closed her eyes. A sensible person would go home and have a salad. But she didn't want to be sensible. Besides, who ate salads in winter? She'd happily heat up some vegetable soup, but lettuce could wait until the weather was warmer.

"Yes, please," she said.

Rochelle rang up the sale, and Anemone tapped her card to pay for it.

"You could go sit in the corner. Our artist in residence is due in soon, and he's very popular. If you're first in line, he might even get your portrait finished in time for you take it with you when you go." Rochelle shooed her toward the corner table. "Go on, I'll bring your order out to you when it's ready."

Reluctantly, Anemone headed for the corner, then changed her mind and took the table next to it. The wall was covered with sketches, both black and white and colour. Mostly people's faces, head and shoulders portraits, some of them drinking coffee or eating cake. There was a whole row of Rochelle, in various poses as she served people at the counter. The artist had captured her smile perfectly, even in the sketches that looked like a few hurried lines.

Maybe she should wait for the artist, and ask him to draw her portrait. An artist's first impression of who she was now – Morgan's widow, Dunstan's lover, or just the café's muffin addict? Maybe a cheesecake addict, if it looked as good as it tasted, she thought as Rochelle approached.

Anemone took her time savouring the cheesecake, which was every bit as good as Rochelle had promised. The Vienna chocolate was too bitter, until she dumped a couple of packets of sugar into it and stirred the cream through, which made it drinkable, if not something she'd order again.

But by the time she'd finished, the sun was almost down, and Dunstan would be waking up.

She cast one last, longing glance at the pictures on the wall, but the mysterious artist who'd drawn them hadn't arrived, and she wanted to tell Dunstan about the police visit before they got too distracted doing other things.

Perhaps she'd get her portrait done tomorrow, or some other night. Dunstan was waiting.

FIFTY

"Have a delightful day, my sweet lass. I'll be back to warm your bed at sundown," Dunstan whispered in her ear. He kissed her neck one last time, and then he was gone, back into the darkness to hide from the dawn.

Anemone eyed the blinds. They were supposed to block out the sun, but two telltale stripes on either side let in the light that drove Dunstan away every morning. Now, if she were to get blockout curtains that went over the window, and covered the sides, maybe she'd be able to wake up beside him, and even make love in the mornings before she went to work. Or all morning, on a Sunday, like this one.

Well, now she was awake, she might as well get up, and use the bathroom.

Anemone made it as far as the sink before nausea overcame her and she spewed up. Wow, that had to be last night's dinner, and that lovely cheesecake, too. There must have been something wrong with the cheesecake, she decided. Or that bitter chocolate.

She rinsed out her mouth and headed to the kitchen for some water before she went back to bed.

The water didn't want to stay down, either.

An hour later, when all she brought up was bile, Anemone lay on the bed, with all the energy of a limp dishrag. It had to have been something from the café. She hadn't been this sick since before Morgan died. When she was still pregnant.

No, she couldn't be.

Anemone fumbled for her phone, to check the calendar. She hadn't really paid much attention to her period with Morgan gone. It wasn't like she could try for another baby, with no husband any more.

Her last period had been six weeks ago. That wasn't possible. Dunstan was a gargoyle, for god's sake. Stone. He didn't get hard-ons like a normal human because he didn't have blood, or any of the other bodily fluids necessary to get a girl pregnant.

Unless…he could…

Six weeks pregnant. Even that wasn't possible. She'd have had to conceive the day before her last period was due, and she and Dunstan hadn't been bonking like rabbits for more than a week.

Well, except that first night, after she'd found Morgan. But that had been one time, and he hadn't actually come, had he?

She didn't know. She'd been so caught up in

her own pleasure, she hadn't even paid attention to his. Oh, he evidently enjoyed what they did, that she was certain of, but if he'd ever…you know…she couldn't say. It's not like he shouted her name the way she screamed his. And he wasn't human, so he didn't go all soft for a bit afterward, like normal men.

But even if he did…getting pregnant on the first time? Without even trying? After she and Morgan had tried for years, and she'd still lost the baby.

She couldn't be pregnant. Not possible.

She still had some pregnancy tests in the bathroom cabinet. As soon as she had enough fluid in her to pee on one, she'd prove once and for all that she was not pregnant with her gargoyle lover's baby.

FIFTY-ONE

The afternoon sun streamed through the bathroom window, haloing the three pregnancy tests Anemone had lined up on the sink. All three said the same thing: that there was nothing wrong with the café's cheesecake, and in a little under eight months, if she was very, very lucky, she'd finally become a mother.

She swept the tests into the bin. She shouldn't get her hopes up. She'd lost the last one, and there was no guarantee she'd be able to carry this baby to term. Maybe she wasn't meant to be a mother. Some people weren't, after all. She had Lucky. That would do her.

But if she could carry this child to term…

Her breath caught in her throat.

She'd do her utmost to be the best mother possible. She wouldn't be perfect, but she'd at least try. It wasn't like she'd be able to have more than one. Just one child would be a miracle.

More than she dared to hope for.

Anemone burst into tears.

She wasn't sure how long it took her to get control of herself, and wipe her eyes and nose, but by the time she did, she had a plan.

She'd visit her doctor during the week for a checkup, to make sure everything was all right, and set up an appointment with the obstetrician she'd chosen last time. But first, she should find the box of baby things she'd bought for the baby she lost. A box she'd brought to the apartment, but hadn't been able to bear to unpack. Until now.

Anemone checked every room in the house, but there was no sign of that box. Could she have stashed it in the storeroom downstairs? She couldn't think where else it could be.

She flicked on the light in the storeroom, and saw why. Beside the box was another one she'd ordered online, which had arrived after she'd lost the baby. It had a picture of a bassinet on the side, with a joyful mother and baby. She'd barely been able to look at it.

Now, she regarded it thoughtfully. She'd done a lot of research, and it had been the best bassinet available then, which meant it would definitely do for this baby. She'd better bring it upstairs now, while she could still lift things, just in case.

She made it across the foyer and halfway up to the landing before she regretted picking up the box. She should have waited and asked Dunstan to carry the damn thing.

"Oh, do you need help with that?"

Catena and a hulking man she didn't know

stood on the landing, staring down at her.

The strong, independent woman in her wanted to say no. But the one who'd thrown up half a dozen times before breakfast won. "Oh, yes, please."

The hulk picked it up in one hand like it weighed nothing, then waited at the top of the stairs, frowning at it, while Anemone dragged herself up afterward.

"Are you having a baby?" Catena exclaimed. "You're barely showing at all! Wow, you must have conceived the last time you and your husband…that's…" She turned an alarming shade of red and shut up.

"Where do you want me to put this?" the hulk asked.

Anemone pushed open the door and pointed down the hall. "Just put it in the guest room, please."

He dropped it off, then returned to stand beside Catena. "We wish you all the best for your health and happiness," he said, his deep frown belying his words, before he wrapped an arm around Catena's shoulders and all but dragged her back into her apartment.

"Tor, that was rude!" Catena scolded, then turned to call over her shoulder, "Sorry about Tor. He's not used to things like good manners and talking to women. We're really very happy for you!"

The door slammed shut behind her.

Anemone stared after them for a long moment, before heading back into her own apartment.

Her neighbour's weird new boyfriend, if that's indeed what he was, definitely wasn't her problem. She had enough to worry about. And maybe even wish for.

FIFTY-TWO

Sex with Anemone was like nothing else Dunstan had ever experienced. As a man, he'd had good sex, or at least he thought he had, but with her…he could go all night, with wave after wave of pleasure washing over both of them. He hadn't thought it would be possible for a gargoyle to experience an orgasm, but with Anemone…it wasn't a question of if, but how many. More than he cared to count, now, because he was too intent on her pleasure, the way her breath caught just before she clenched down hard and screamed his name.

He could go all night, but she was still human, so she needed sleep. Reluctantly, he pulled out of her and cleaned them both up. The shimmer in her eyes as she stared up at him…if he didn't know better, he'd think it was love. But he'd never known a woman who was capable of love, no matter how many times she said she was. Anemone had never spoken of love, and he'd never known her to lie, which made her superior to most of the women he'd met.

Yet when he heard someone shouting his name from the rooftop, he knew he had to answer. But he waited until Anemone had drifted off to sleep before he left her side to find out who was making so much noise.

A hulking man stood on the other side of the fence that separated Anemone's section of the rooftop from her neighbour's. A familiar shape, though Dunstan couldn't summon a single memory that would tell him the man's name.

"How do you know me?" Dunstan demanded. He might not remember, but the other man might.

"You are my brother."

"Ben?" So much hope in that one syllable, only for it to be dashed when the other man shook his head.

"Torstan."

He knew the name, but memories of the man were slow to surface. Perhaps if he could see the man's face… "Step into the light, so I can see you, brother." If indeed this man was his brother.

Torstan leaped lightly over the low fence, so the beam of the streetlight struck his face.

Yes, it was familiar, but…

"You're still cursed," Torstan said. "A gargoyle still. I thought you must be a man, to have fathered a child, but…how?"

A child. He remembered talk of a child, though he had never seen the boy. "Cara. She gave my son to Oscar when she married him." Memories surfaced, of Cara's face, as she told him she'd chosen his best friend instead of him to be her husband, even when the child was Dunstan's. She'd spoken of love, but it had been a lie.

"That's a lie. You never let me say a bad word about Cara, even as you pined for her loss, but she was a lying whore who double crossed you and Oscar both. The boy she gave birth to was Oscar's son. I'd swear it on our father's grave. She met him in the quarry every day for months, moaning like a mad ghost as she fucked him. It was only a matter of time before she got pregnant, and she married him, like she wanted. Then you came home, and she threw Oscar's proposal in his face after you seduced her. Then she came to tell you about the babe, swearing it was yours, screaming about how you'd promised to marry her, but you'd already gone back to sea. I had to call her a liar, to send her to beg Oscar to take her back. The poor man married her, harpy that she was, and you dodged a bullet with that one. So don't talk to me about Cara."

Dunstan didn't understand. "Then what child are you talking about?"

"The one the widow carries in her belly. Your child, for it cannot belong to her dead husband. We came to warn her about you, but we were already too late, weren't we? You'd seduced her, just like you seduced Cara. God damn you, Dunstan, she was still a widow in mourning!"

That first night he'd made love to Anemone, and every amazing night since. These memories were crystal clear. Every breathy moan, every desperate plea for more…if he'd seduced Anemone, she'd seduced him right back.

"It wasn't like that. Me and Anemone, we…" Fell in love? He wanted to deny that it was possible, but the moment he'd thought the words, they felt right. That didn't mean he'd blurt them out to this man. The man who claimed to be his brother, blaming him for…

"Did you say Anemone is pregnant?"

"Of course, you fool! What do you think happens when you bed a woman?"

"How do you know?" How could this stranger possibly know when Dunstan himself didn't?

"Because Catena and I saw her today, carrying a cradle upstairs for the baby. And where were you?"

Dunstan closed his eyes. In the dark, hiding from the sun, when he should have been helping her.

"She's not Cara. This is a good woman, and you can still make an honest woman of her. You go back down there now, and marry her, like you should, instead of running away to sea. Be a father to your own child, though God only knows what a half gargoyle baby will look like. Marry her, before she has the sense to find someone else, like Cara did, to be a real father, to provide for her and the child." Torstan shook his head. "You were supposed to protect her, not seduce her. No wonder you haven't broken the curse, if you couldn't even protect her from yourself."

Of course he'd protected her. From the ceiling collapsing, and then helping catch her husband's killers. He'd held her when she cried, been there for her whenever she needed him. Even in bed, it had been her need that had called him to her, and he couldn't deny her. Couldn't deny her anything.

If Anemone was really carrying his child…

He looked up, but Torstan had gone. Some brother, judging him then disappearing before he could defend himself.

To hell with him. This was between him, and Anemone.

He would return to her, and wait until she woke. Then he'd ask her, and if what Torstan told him was true, then…she would make him the happiest man alive.

FIFTY-THREE

When Anemone opened her eyes, she found Dunstan staring at her.

"Good morning," she said, then sat up so she could see the clock. Five am? Oh, no, that was far too early to be awake. "I take that back. I need more sleep."

"Please."

She opened her eyes again. He was still staring at her. "What?"

"Is it true? Are you carrying my child?"

She sighed. She'd wanted to wait until she'd seen the doctor, to make sure everything was okay, but... "I think so. I took a pregnancy test, and it came back positive, but seeing as I lost the last one, I wasn't certain. I've made a doctor's appointment on Monday, so she can check if everything's all right. I wasn't going to say anything until she confirmed it, but…how on Earth did you find out? Is it some sort of secret gargoyle power you haven't told me about?"

"Torstan told me."

"My neighbour's grumpy new boyfriend?" If she hadn't liked him before, she was seriously pissed at him now. "He's an arsehole."

"He's my brother."

She blinked. "Poor you."

Dunstan laughed. "He ordered me to marry you."

"A huge, nosy, interfering arsehole whose arse I am totally going to kick when I see him next. What business is it of his?"

"It doesn't matter. He's right. If you're going to be the mother of my child, then I want to marry you. To provide for you and the baby. Not just protect you. I'll need to find a job, and learn how to live in this time."

"Do I get a say in this?"

Dunstan stared at her. "But I thought you'd be happy. Isn't that what every woman wants — a man who will take care of her, while she has their children?"

"I don't know — I've never had children. I might be a terrible mother. I might not even be able to carry a child to term. I mean, I know I wanted children. I wanted a family. I just…gave up when Morgan died. Now I've only had a few hours to get used to the idea that it might be possible again, and you're talking about marriage? I…it's five am!" Anemone closed her eyes. She was babbling, and even she didn't know what she wanted. Well, Dunstan, obviously. And the baby, if fate would allow her to keep it. "Ask me again when the baby is born. When we know he or she is safe and healthy and ours. And…will be able to walk down the aisle in front of us at the wedding." Now she had the image in her head of a chubby toddler in a white dress, clutching a bunch of flowers. Or would it be a little ringbearer in an adorable suit?

"You don't want to marry me?" His voice sounded even, but she could see the hurt in his eyes.

Anemone sighed. "This is crazy. I've only known you a few weeks, but I already can't imagine my life without you. I'm pretty sure I'm in love with you. So, fuck, yeah, I want to marry you. But not before this baby can walk. This isn't Victorian times. We can have a baby together without being married, and work things out as we go along. Oh, except the sex. Pretty sure we've got that figured out, and I want a lot more of that. Right up to the third trimester, if I remember correctly. And afterwards, obviously."

Dunstan was still staring at her. "I don't think I've ever met a woman quite like you,

Anemone Seaver."

"Well, if I marry you, I might not be Anemone Seaver for much longer. What is your last name anyway? I don't think you've ever told me."

He paused, then said. "Stone. Dunstan Stone."

"Figures. A gargoyle called Stone. I could live with that." She took a deep breath. "Dunstan Stone, father of the child I'm carrying, will you marry me, when this baby learns to walk?"

"If that is what you wish, then yes. Of course I will."

She smiled. "Actually, right now, what I wish is that we could make love again before the sun comes up. Dawn isn't until seven, so maybe…"

Dunstan flipped her onto her back, then loomed over her, before leaning in for a kiss. "For my betrothed, I shall see that you have three orgasms before the sun rises."

And he proceeded to give her all that, and

more.

FIFTY-FOUR

"Do we have to invite them over for dinner?" Dunstan complained.

"Yes. I promised Catena I'd make her dinner ages ago, for helping me out, and he's your brother. We should probably announce our engagement, so he'll stop glowering all the time. Or maybe that's just his normal expression, and your brother is a grumpy git."

Someone knocked at the door. "Right, that'll

be them. Do you want to answer it?"

Dunstan headed off, then returned a minute later with Catena and Tor…Torstan…whatever his name was in tow.

"Anemone, this is my younger brother, Torstan. Tor, this is my betrothed, Anemone. She wishes to kick your arse for gossiping about her baby, but, given her condition, I intend to do it for her." Dunstan advanced on his brother.

"Stop!" Catena stood between them, one hand resting on each man's chest. "What have I told you about fighting?"

To Anemone's surprise, Tor hung his head. "Not even outside?"

"No!"

There was some grumbling, but Tor took a seat at the table, and the others joined him.

Anemone checked the oven timer. She had twenty minutes – time to sit down and have a glass of…well, not wine for her, but something, anyway.

"So, are you a gargoyle, too?" she asked Tor.

"Not any more. Catena broke the curse."

Anemone stared. "It's a curse? How do you break it?"

Catena turned red. "Um…it's…the spell book said something about melting a heart of stone. Tor's curse broke the morning after we had sex for the first time." She coughed. "Obviously, that wasn't the case with you two, if he's still a gargoyle. So…I guess you'll need to try something different." Her cheeks grew even redder.

"Like whipped cream and sprinkles," Tor suggested.

Catena looked like she wanted to dive under the table and hide.

Anemone hid her smile. Best if she change the subject before the poor girl died of embarrassment. "So, do you have any more gargoyle brothers I should know about?"

Tor and Dunstan exchanged a glance.

"Have you seen Ben?" Dunstan asked.

Tor shook his head. "He was there with us

that night. First he took you away, then me, but I don't know what happened to Ben. If he was buried beneath this house, like we were, surely he should have been awoken when we were, but…"

They turned to the girls. "Is there any way to find out what happened?"

Catena shrugged. "Well, if he was a convict like you two, there might be something in the prison records. That's Anemone's department, not mine, though."

Anemone froze. Dunstan hadn't told her he was a convict. He'd hardly told her anything about his past. No wonder, if the father of her child was a criminal. "Let me get my computer," she heard herself say, and hurried out of the room. In the study, she took a moment to breathe through the panic and compose herself before she returned to the table with her laptop.

She logged into the database, then asked, "What's your brother's name?"

"Ben Stone," Tor said.

Anemone typed it in, then hit enter.

She stared at the record for a long moment. There wasn't much, but it was enough. "It says here he died in 1855."

"That's not possible!"

"He was right there with us. He had to be turned into a gargoyle, too!"

"He was going to study art. He was so good. Paint, pencil, stone…he could draw to life, and make you believe a statue was ready to step off the plinth, it looked so real. I remember the statue of a girl he carved for Burke Castle, she looked like she was about to open her eyes any moment…"

"Ben can't be dead. He just can't be. Check it again." Dunstan's eyes begged her, and Anemone clicked on the record to see if there was any more.

There was the date of his arrival, and the date of his death. And his crime: murder.

"I'm sorry," Anemone said. "There's nothing else here. It says he died in June 1855."

While the brothers expressed their disbelief and grief all over again, Anemone clicked on the search box. This time, she just typed STONE and hit enter.

Three names came up. Only one had a death date, but all three had the same arrival date, and they'd been convicted of the same crime.

Anemone closed her eyes. She'd slept with a convicted killer. How could she have been so stupid? All the signs had been there. The number of times he'd offered to inflict violence on people for her, to avenge Morgan's killer…what he'd done to that catamaran…

"Yeah, your brother's dead, and I'm sorry, but you both have some explaining to do." She turned the screen around so they could all see it. "Care to explain how you were convicted of murder and weren't hanged for it?"

Tor and Dunstan exchanged glances. "We didn't do it. Wrongfully accused, wrongfully convicted…we never even touched her. We weren't even home, but they found her body in our cottage, so…"

Catena's hand touched Anemone's wrist. "If he's still cursed, and your protector, you can command him to tell you the truth. He won't be able to lie."

Anemone closed her eyes. She didn't want to believe he was a murderer, but she didn't want to give him orders, either. It was all kinds of wrong. But she couldn't marry a murderer.

"Dunstan," she begged, wishing he could fix this. "The truth?"

He hung his head. "She's right. Command me to tell the truth, and I must. I already have, but if you need to hear it again. I love you, and I would never hurt you. I've never hurt a woman in my life, and I never will. I might have punched a man or two, but I've never killed one."

She stared into his eyes for a long moment. She wanted to believe him, so much.

"What about Tor?"

"He never killed anyone, either."

"And Ben?"

Dunstan sighed. "He was in love with her. He wanted to marry her, to take her as his wife to the Swan River Colony. We would have helped him, but…she died. Nobody knows who did it."

Tor's frown deepened. "I warrant Ben knows, or he did."

Dunstan's hand landed on Anemone's. She didn't move away. "Please, Anemone. We need to find out what happened to Ben. If he really died that day or…whatever you can discover. Are there other records that you can't access with that thing?" He waved at the laptop.

She blew out a breath. "Yes, there are records at the prison that haven't yet been digitised. I can go through them, and see what I can find about your brother."

"Even if it's just where he's buried, so we can pay our respects," Tor said.

Anemone couldn't deny them that. "All right. Tomorrow, I'll see what I can find for you. But if the database says he's dead, don't get your hopes up. Even with modern medicine, people rarely live past a hundred."

The brothers exchanged a look of deep sadness. "He was the best of us. You should have seen his artwork. Maybe some of that survived, even if he didn't. You never know…"

"You never know."

FIFTY-FIVE

"Good evening. One cinnamon roll and a double shot espresso for my protector, as promised," Rochelle announced as she set her tray down on the table. "What are you working on?"

"Today's masterpiece," he said, holding up the sketch.

"I do not stick my tongue out like that!"

"Sure you do. Whenever you're doing a

design in the froth on top of a cappuccino, you stick the tip of your tongue out, just like that. I'm going to add it to the collection." He pinned it to the wall, next to all the other sketches he'd done of her.

Rochelle shook her head. "If you and Tacey hadn't sworn you were here to be my protector at night, I'd wonder if you're a stalker. I mean, that many pictures of me is a bit much."

He shrugged. "When the café is quiet, and it's just you and me here, I take my inspiration from you. I believe I shall call today's piece BLEP." He scrawled the letters beneath the picture, and underlined them.

Rochelle had to laugh. "You're a nutter, all right, but they do say great art requires at least a little bit of crazy. Ooh, look, we have a customer. For you or for me?"

He pulled out his portfolio. "For me, I think. I have a commission for him."

Rochelle returned to the counter.

"Is that mine?" the man asked eagerly. "Oh, it's beautiful. You've got the fish scales just right. It's better than the photo."

The artist smiled indulgently. "Why thank you."

The man pulled out his wallet and paid him, but he didn't put it away. "Actually, I wanted to ask if you could do some pictures of my kids in the same style, so I could frame them. My wife and me are divorced, and I only get to see them on weekends. I could show you some pictures…" He pulled out his phone and started swiping.

The artist held up his hand. "I'd be happy to do portraits of your children, but I must see them first. Pictures are all good and well, but they don't have the same life as the presence of a real person. Bring your kids into the café one evening when I'm working, and I'll do it."

The man put his wallet and phone away. "Oh, I will. This is beautiful. I'll tell all my mates at work about you, too." He squinted at the artist's signature. "What did you say your name is again?"

"Ben. Ben Stone. Evening artist in residence at the Shut Up Café," the artist said.

ABOUT THE AUTHOR

Demelza Carlton has always loved the ocean, but on her first snorkelling trip she found she was afraid of fish.

She has since swum with sea lions, sharks and sea cucumbers and stood on spray drenched cliffs over a seething sea as a seven-metre cyclonic swell surged in, shattering a shipwreck below.

Demelza now lives in Perth, Western Australia, the shark attack capital of the world.

The *Ocean's Gift* series was her first foray into fiction, followed by her suspense thriller *Nightmares* trilogy. She swears the *Mel Goes to Hell* series ambushed her on a crowded train and wouldn't leave her alone.

Want to know more? You can follow Demelza on Facebook, Twitter, YouTube or her website, Demelza Carlton's Place at:

www.demelzacarlton.com

Books by Demelza Carlton

Siren of Secrets series
Ocean's Secret (#1)
Ocean's Gift (#2)
Ocean's Infiltrator (#3)

Siren of War series
Ocean's Justice (#1)
Ocean's Widow (#2)
Ocean's Bride (#3)
Ocean's Rise (#4)
Ocean's War (#5)
How To Catch Crabs

Nightmares Trilogy
Nightmares of Caitlin Lockyer (#1)
Necessary Evil of Nathan Miller (#2)
Afterlife of Alana Miller (#3)

Mel Goes to Hell series
The Devil's Work (#1)
See You in Hell (#2)
Mel Goes to Hell (#3)
To Hell and Back (#4)
The Holiday From Hell (#5)
All Hell Breaks Loose (#6)
The Devil Goes to Heaven (#7)

Romance Island Resort series

Maid for the Rock Star (#1)
The Rock Star's Email Order Bride (#2)
The Rock Star's Virginity (#3)
The Rock Star and the Billionaire (#4)
The Rock Star Wants A Wife (#5)
The Rock Star's Wedding (#6)
Maid for the South Pole (#7)

Romance a Medieval Fairytale series

Enchant: Beauty and the Beast Retold
Dance: Cinderella Retold
Fly: Goose Girl Retold
Revel: Twelve Dancing Princesses Retold
Silence: Little Mermaid Retold
Awaken: Sleeping Beauty Retold
Embellish: Brave Little Tailor Retold
Appease: Princess and the Pea Retold
Blow: Three Little Pigs Retold
Return: Hansel and Gretel Retold
Wish: Aladdin Retold
Melt: Snow Queen Retold
Spin: Rumpelstiltskin Retold
Kiss: Frog Prince Retold
Reflect: Snow White Retold
Roar: Goldilocks Retold
Cobble: Elves and the Shoemaker Retold
Float: Enchanted Horse Retold
Steal: Forty Thieves Retold
Call: Pied Piper Retold

Feather: Swan Maidens Retold
Curse: Rose Red Retold
Cross: Three Billy Goats Gruff Retold
Weave: Rapunzel Retold
Claim: Puss in Boots Retold

Colony Universe

Cowboys and Aliens
Ghost
Vulcan
Cupid
Valentine
Prometheus
Halcyon
Poseidon
Apollo

Heart of Stone series

Broken Chains
Broken Bonds
Broken Dreams

Heart of Steel series

Stone Guardian
Stone Champion
Stone Sentinel
Stone Shadow